KONRAD

LEANN ASHERS

Konrad

Copyright © 2021 by LeAnn Ashers
All rights reserved.
Konrad is a work of fiction. Names, characters, places, and incidents are all products of the author's imagination and are used fictitiously. Any resemblance to actual events, locales, or persons, living or dead, is entirely coincidental.
Except as permitted under the US Copyright Act of 1976, no part of this publication may be reproduced, distributed, or transmitted in any form, by any means, or stored in a database or retrieval system without the prior written permission of the author.
Cover Designer: Regina Wamba
Photographer: Wander Aguiar
Editor: Aquila Editing

1

ETTA

TWENTY-FOUR YEARS OLD

I smile at the girls as I help them get settled into their new rooms, their new clothes, and their new life.

Their faces show exactly what mine did five years ago when I was eighteen years old, when my brother took me out of a cult.

My job now is to save those who need out. I take care of them and help them transfer into the real world. It's such a life-changing thing, even to this day sometimes I have a hard time.

But I am here for them, whatever it takes.

The MC has given me free rein to do whatever is needed to take care of the girls. We have a hotline that girls can call if they are in trouble and we've gone nationwide.

I've been doing this since I was eighteen, when the MC took in the girls that belonged to the cult I was in.

My stomach is twisted in knots at the thought of some of these girls being forced into this. There are some that can't be saved and they're suffering in this very moment.

It's hard doing this, mostly mentally. I see things that give me nightmares, and it brings up old memories, but knowing I am making a difference is so worth it.

I was married at fourteen years old. My sister Lynn was married at thirteen and she had a two-year-old daughter by the time she was sixteen.

My husband was extremely abusive. He sent me back to my parents in hopes that they could fix me.

Nothing could have fixed me. I had spirit and a will to fight him. I never had a child. I'm forever thankful for that because I've helped my sister Lynn raise her daughter.

For as long as I can remember I've been abused, by my father, my mother, and other family members.

Cults are built on it.

Religion is their way of justifying it. They take verses in the Bible and twist them for their benefit. It's their way of using their sick fantasies and making them normal.

It's taken years but we are known countrywide for the work we do.

The Grim Sinners MC and the Devil Souls MC started this. They supply the funds, but in the last year people from around the world have donated to make sure we can help everyone.

We started a new fostering program and we're allowing some of the teenage girls to go and stay in foster homes if they want so they can have space from all of the other girls. We only allow people with links to the MC to foster the girls and we have a rigorous vetting process.

Lynn, my sister, is twenty-two and a counselor. She specialized in this. Together we are changing the world, we are speaking on the way we grew up and how this is happening right under everyone's noses.

Not anymore.

Tonight I'm going on a mission with the Grim Sinners MC. We received word that a thirteen-year-old girl is being married off to a deacon in her church and the Grim Sinners are joining me to go get her and any others we come across.

I spoke to Lane in great length on the information she has

given me, but she had to hang up because she had to get breakfast ready for her family.

Her wedding is tomorrow so it has to happen tonight or we may lose her, forever.

Lynn walks into the main house where I am, holding her daughter's hand. Michaela smiles widely when she sees me.

"Hi sweet girl, how was school today?" I ask her and pull her into my arms, hugging her tight.

She squeezes me tightly; she is truly the sweetest little girl. "It was okay. I'm starving."

I laugh and smooth down the back of her hair. "Tell the cook to make you a snack before dinner, sweetheart."

She takes off running and I look at my sister. "Are you ready for tonight?"

She nods, throwing her hair over her shoulder. "I am. I'll probably stay in the apartment upstairs tonight because I don't know how long it will take once you bring her here."

Lynn is the person who helps get everyone adjusted emotionally. That's the most important part, honestly. The internal fight is the biggest struggle. You are so brainwashed, trained to think a certain way, you just can't help but fight yourself.

The bravery of these women astounds me—it takes extraordinary courage to take a chance, reach out to me, knowing if they're caught the consequences would be dire.

"That's a good idea. Rosie is struggling also. I heard her crying in the bathroom if you want to check on her."

Lynn hugs me and moves through the house to Rosie's room. She was rescued last week after she was forced to marry her uncle. It was a complete surprise to her and she finally had a chance to call us a week after she was married. She was his eighteenth wife.

Michaela, now seven, was three when my brother took us

out of that life. She was young enough that she wasn't affected and I'm thankful for that more than anything.

My phone buzzes, letting me know that the guys are driving through the gate. "Lynn, I'm leaving!" I yell up the stairs and grab my bag, running outside.

I'm confident in my training. I was trained by a Navy SEAL that trained some of the guys in the MC. It was not like their training at all, but I can shoot and I can defend myself—and someone else if it came down to it.

Three large SUVs pull to a stop in front of the building. Lane gets out, with Smiley and Wilder, and then I can't stop the grin when I see my brother Vinny get out also.

He almost always joins me to make sure I'm safe. This hits close for him also. The cults deeply affect him just as much as they do me.

He comes around and hugs me. "How are the twins?" I ask.

He gives me that dopey smile that lets me know he's living his best life. "They're great. It's hard to believe they're turning five years old." He shakes his head in disbelief.

My heart aches with happiness, but I long to have my own kids someday. "I can't wait to see them tomorrow."

"We'll stop before we reach the location to put your vest on, Etta."

I smile at Smiley. "Thank you, Smiley."

His wife is like a mom to me. She's here practically every day, mothering everyone here to make sure they're okay.

Smiley motions for me to get into the front seat. I hand him my bag as I climb inside.

I take out my phone to text the girl to tell her we are leaving and we will be there in a few hours.

We can sneak her out, but we've learned that sometimes it's easier to just bust down the door.

It sends a message that we aren't afraid and lets others know we mean business. We want to be feared, we want the girls or boys being abused to know that we are here and no matter what we will be there.

The drive there is mostly silent, besides the guys talking about club business, which I tune out because I learned a long time ago to mind my business when it comes to such things.

The closer we get, the lights grow darker and darker. The houses are all the same—the same style, the same colors, and no decorations.

Lane pulls over to the side of the road. I step out and Vinny hands me my bulletproof vest, slipping it over my head and securing it.

"Be safe, Etta. Don't do anything stupid, yeah?" He says this every single time, and I nod, but I know I would do whatever it takes to protect these kids.

Smiley comes around wearing his very own vest. The guys all still have their cut on. He hands me a pistol with a holster, and I bend over and strap it around my right thigh for easy reach.

I bend over and throw my hair into a bun at the top of my head, letting out a deep breath.

I smile at the guys who are staring at me. I know they're concerned, worried, but this is what I do. I've done this over a hundred times.

I am meant to do this.

No one protected us when we were kids; we didn't have a savior. Me, Lynn, Vinny, and Danny, we all suffered, and my brother protected us as long as he could.

"Let's do this."

They get inside and I don't bother buckling my seat belt. We're only minutes away. She texted me with an *okay* earlier. I can't imagine how scared she is and I know the wait is excruciating.

My first thought when I pull up to her house is there is a

shitload of people there. Fear runs through me. "Fuck, they must have started the wedding early!"

My heart is pounding so hard in my chest because I'm so scared for her. I know what she's feeling right now, the absolutely terrifying feeling of knowing that your life is going to be so much worse.

You're already not your own person, but then adding on a husband? To them, in God's eyes, the men fully control you.

It's hell.

I see the hell in every single woman and child. The future is unknown, but the hope is still there in the back of their minds.

The guys cuss and we step out. Wilder runs behind the house to make sure they don't try to run out of the back with her. We have had that happen before but we caught up with them.

It's been a major learning curve from the start. We learned the hard way but we didn't make that same mistake twice.

Asking nicely does not work—a gun in the face usually does the trick.

Vinny runs right up to the door, kicking it in. I follow right behind Vinny, with the guys at my side and my back.

I hear a scream the second we step over the threshold. Women are clutching their chests and the men are staring at us.

Right in the middle of the living room is a thirteen-year-old girl in a white dress with a man old enough to be her grandfather; he looks fucking disgusting.

Her eyes seek me out from the group of men surrounding me. I give her a nod and a slight smile, letting her know that I'm here.

Her face is stained with tears and mascara, and she looks disgusted by the sick look on her would-be groom's face as he smiles at her. She's dressed like an adult, but it doesn't cover up the fact that she's a baby.

I let out a deep breath as it sinks in. We're here in time.

"We are here for the girl," I tell everyone in the room.

Silence, then the groom grabs her arm hard. The girl winces as she bends almost half at the tightness of his grip.

She looks at me with pure panic on her face. My stomach twists at the sight of the fear. The guys beside me take a step forward just as I do, preparing for a brawl. Everyone is just staring at us.

I pull my gun out of the holster, clicking off the safety and pointing it at the old fucker. "Release her, now," I demand, my voice unwavering, my eyes trained on his every move.

I hear a bunch of women gasp dramatically and a few of the men shift in their seats, unsure of what to do.

The pastor, and the oldest guy in the room by far, steps from around them, moving closer to me, and the guys shift a little closer to me.

"Satan's disciples are not welcome here, Jezebel." He spits the last word and I try not to laugh.

I can't count the number of times I get called that. I smirk at him. His steps falter at my smile. I am not a member of his church; his words mean nothing. "Let her go," I demand once again.

The girl is shaking from head to toe, her eyes pleading with me.

A woman and man step forward in front of us. "We are her parents. She has our permission to marry," the man who I assume is her father tells us.

I glare at them and all I feel is hatred. "Did she give permission? Did she want this? Did she want to be married to some shriveled up old cock? No, she fucking didn't. She is thirteen years old. Her life should be about sports and spending time with her friends. Not being a fucking wife, where she will be abused every day of her life and forced to have children." I unleash my fury on them.

The father's face changes to so many different shades of red as I speak my mind, everyone in the room going silent as my words sink in.

But no one in this room has argued different. Their lives are hell.

"Give me the girl or I won't be responsible for my actions." My voice is clear, leaving no room for arguments.

The pedo tightens his hand on her, causing her to cry out in pain. I smile. "Big mistake."

I lower my gun, pointing to his knee, and pull the trigger. His face shows his shock just before he hits the ground like a pile of lead, screaming at the top of his lungs.

People start crying, and the men stand like they are going to do something. She takes off running to me and her father swoops in at the last second and grabs her.

Hell no.

I step up and grab his arm, bending it up his back, and with one solid pull I break his arm. I throw him to the ground and his wife falls next to him.

I take the girl's hand and pull her to me. She clings to me like her life depends on it—and in her case it does.

"This is not over," the pastor calls out as I turn my back to the room.

I look at him over my shoulder. "It will never be over until all of you are dead." The room is silent once more as my words sink in.

I will never rest. I will never settle until every single one of these fuckers is dead.

I SIT in back with her on the way back while she cries and clutches my hand with all of her might.

"I just want you to know how brave you are..." I trail off, not knowing her name.

She wipes under her eyes. I reach into my bag and pull out a makeup wipe for her. "My name is Linda." She finally gives me her name.

"I am so glad you got to me when you did. He married one of my friends who was a couple years older than me and she died in childbirth. I was nine and she was twelve when she married him."

I hate that this happened. "I'm glad I got there in time too. You won't ever have to worry about them ever again."

She smiles. "I'm thankful for that. I've read in books what it's like to be a teenager. I want that."

"You will have all of that. You have so many options in life now."

She smiles. "My parents weren't mean to me. I will miss them but I won't forgive them for forcing me to marry."

I imagine the betrayal of her parents hurts her deeply no matter how great of parents they were. "I grew up in a cult also. I was forced to marry when I was fourteen years old. My sister Lynn was your age. I understand."

Her eyes flash and I can tell she sees me in a new light. "I never would have thought."

"My brother Vinny." I nod my head in his direction. "He did also, but he ran away when he was very young."

"Is it okay if I take a nap? I haven't slept in days since I got the news." I reach behind me and take a blanket out of the back. "I have some friends who want out also—can you help them too?"

I nod, and she leans against the door with the blanket tucked under her neck. The ride back to the houses is silent as everyone lets her get much-needed sleep.

We pull up in front of the gate. Lane inputs the code and we drive down the long driveway, passing houses all the way to the big house.

"Wake up, honey. We're here." I put my hand on Linda's shoulder gently to not scare her.

Her eyes flutter open and she sits straight up and looks out of the window, taking in everything as the main house comes into view. It's a literal mansion. The MC built this and the money shows through.

"This is where I'll be staying?" she asks, her face showing her awe.

I smile. "This will be your home as long as you want it."

Some of the girls here are so severely abused that they will never recover and they have accepted the peace and safety here.

Peace is something I understand completely. Some things you can't move on from, but if they are happy then that is what matters the most.

The women who don't want to be reintroduced to society have small houses on the back of the property where they live. They all take care of each other and we take care of them.

If we can give them peace, then that's what matters the most, right?

We pull to a stop and Lynn walks outside to greet us. She's wearing her best smile—the one she reserves for the girls.

I step out and hold the door open for her. "Lynn, this is Linda. Linda, this is my sister Lynn."

Lynn steps closer. "It's so nice to meet you. Come with me, I'll show you your room." Linda takes Lynn's hand and they slip inside of the house.

I turn my attention to the guys. I feel unfulfilled. "We have to go back. We've not dealt with them at all yet."

Vinny nods. "I agree. I got really bad vibes from them."

"How about once she's feeling better we'll get together and discuss plans?" Lane suggests.

"I like that idea. Goodnight. See you tomorrow, Vinny." I give my brother a hug and slip inside of the house, exhausted but burning to do more.

2

THE NEXT DAY

Today is my niece and nephew's birthday. They're twins and are turning five. They were born a few months after I came to live with my brother.

I walk up the driveway to the backyard. The twins, Sariah and Caleb, spot me and run over. "Wow, those are for us?" Sariah's eyes are glowing as she looks at the big presents.

I know I went overboard, but they're my babies. I don't have any kids, but in my heart I love them as I would love my own and Michaela.

"Mommy, look! Look what Etta gave me!" Caleb runs ahead with the present. Sariah is struggling holding hers. Trey takes the present from Caleb, and I move to help Sariah when Caleb runs back to take it from her.

I spot Lynn getting out of her SUV. I walk to her so we can walk inside the gate together. We both tend to get nervous around people we don't know.

We all know no one will hurt us, especially the guys that are in the MC—I know all of them—but we have some random parents we don't know here from the twins' school.

There is one guy named Lee. He is an uncle of one of the

kids that go to school with the twins. He comes everywhere with the parents.

I don't like him.

I don't like the way he stares at me and Lynn, but me in particular. I seem to get most of his focus, which I'm thankful for because that means the focus is off of Lynn. He tries to talk to me, but I always manage to slip past him.

I haven't told anyone because he hasn't done anything to me, plus I only ever see him at school functions and things like that. I just don't like his vibes.

"Hey sister, how is Linda?" I ask Lynn once she walks up to me. Michaela runs past us to go play with the kids, her long, beautiful hair flowing behind her.

The door to the house opens and Lane walks out with a few of his members. He's speaking to one I've never met before.

He stops talking to Lane and his eyes connect with mine. My stomach flips, my fingers tingle from his gaze. I can't stop the smile that I give him, my face burning from his gaze.

Then he smiles at me. I have to look away and Lynn is grinning from ear to ear at our interaction. "Stop that!" I hiss, trying to gather my senses.

I have never acted like that before. Most of the time when I'm around the guys it's strictly brotherly.

This was different. I felt like I was a teenager and I just spotted a cute boy.

"Cute" is not a word that I would give that guy. He has dark brown hair, with some graying at the temples. Tattoos everywhere, up to under his chin, down his arms, fully sleeved and around six foot five. He's huge.

"Girl, I saw that look between the both of you! Konrad is a great guy," Lynn whispers to me so no one hears. We've walked to the side so we can talk amongst ourselves.

My eyes open wider. "Wait, you know him?" I ask.

She nods. "He volunteers with the boys. He takes them out for the day sometimes."

I can't deny the pleasure I feel that he is kind enough to do that. Lynn smiles again, giving me a weird look.

"Stopppp it." I push her shoulder slightly, my face growing redder.

Lynn giggles, covering her mouth, Vinny walks over to us and I smile at him. "How does it feel the babies being five?" I ask when he gets closer.

"It's fucking hard. One second they were small enough to hold them in one hand and the next they're tearing down the house." Vinny stares into space as he thinks of his babies.

I'm so proud of the person he has become. He has come so far from everything that happened to us as kids, and so has Danny.

Vinny moves closer and has a secret grin on his face. Oh no. "So, I saw that look." Lynn almost falls to the ground in laughter, my face is burning so bad from the embarrassment. Who all saw that? I am such a dork! Why did I smile like that?

"Shut up," I hiss, itching to punch him on the shoulder.

He laughs. "Etta, you almost knocked him on his ass. When you looked away, he grabbed the damn banister."

My embarrassment goes out of the window. "That makes me feel better."

Lynn wraps her arm around my shoulder. "I love you, Etta."

My heart does a little happy dance. "I love you too."

"I'm going to go use the bathroom." I hug her back and tap Vinny on the shoulder. I keep my head down and walk inside of the house, not wanting to look stupid again.

I shut the door behind me, locking it, then look at myself in the mirror, studying myself. In my old life, being pretty made everything harder. If someone was attracted to you, it was your fault because you tempted them.

My husband is alive. We were not legally married. I know

that Vinny tried to find him, but they never could, or Lynn's husband for that matter.

I do have that fear in the back of my mind that he could find me, but it's been years and I doubt that they would even know where to look. What could he do? I'm surrounded by the MC every day of my life.

I was actually kicked out of my home that I slept at—I wouldn't even say I lived there. I survived; his dogs were treated better than I was.

One day I was tired of it. I stood up for myself and I was sent back to my parents so my behavior could be corrected.

Sometimes when I wake up in the morning it's almost like I'm there once again. I have that startling fear for a split second before I come to my senses.

The thing is, we didn't know that this wasn't normal. The life in the cult is made to seem like we were the only normal people in the world. The outside was just made up of sinners and demons.

We just knew that life was shitty and that was the way it was meant to be, until my sister had Michaela.

That's when we knew that we needed to get out. We were planning it, but then Vinny showed up out of nowhere and took us out of there.

I smile at myself in the mirror, letting some of my anxiety melt away. Why was I looking away, being embarrassed? That was not me, not anymore.

I open the bathroom door, and standing right outside of it is Lee.

Oh no.

Konrad

"Who is she?" I ask Lane the second we break eye contact. I can see the blush on her face all the way over here.

Lane chuckles. "She's Etta."

Then it clicks because I've heard the guys talk about her a lot over the years but I've never met her, though I have met Lynn, her sister.

"She's fucking beautiful, man," I confess, looking at her again. She has beautiful blonde hair that reaches her ass, a beautiful tan, and she's tall—around five foot seven or eight.

"Tough as fucking nails," Wilder pipes in.

Lynn looks over at me and smirks, catching me staring at her sister, and Vinny does the same, but I don't give a fuck.

Etta hugs them both and walks inside of the house, keeping her head down as she walks inside.

A minute later I notice a guy practically running inside of the house after her. "I don't fucking like that," I tell Lane.

I walk inside right behind him with Lane and see him standing right outside the bathroom.

Etta

"Can I speak to you for a few minutes?" Lee asks, taking a step closer to me, and I take a step back from him.

I study his body language. He's anxious and looking around to see if anyone is around.

"I'm sorry, but I don't feel comfortable speaking to you right now," I tell him nicely and I step past him, walking through the house in case he changes his mind about letting me pass.

Turning the corner, I spot Lane and Konrad. I make my way to them, instantly feeling relieved. I don't know Konrad, but I know Lane very well. "Are you okay, Etta?" Lane asks.

I nod. "Yeah, I'm fine. I think that guy is a little weird though," I answer honestly.

Konrad looks behind me. I peek around and see Lee just standing there watching the three of us. I can see that he's angry. "I think it's best you go outside to the party," Konrad says to him.

Lee walks past us. I have to take a step back so he doesn't brush against me. A shiver wracks my body.

"I'm going to speak to your brother about this." Lane leaves me and Konrad alone together in the house.

"Thank you for watching out for me," I tell him, feeling kind of nervous being alone with him like this.

His face changes from that deep menacing one that he was giving Lee to one that is different, softer. "It's not a thing, sweetheart."

I try not to close my eyes, his deep voice and that endearment affecting me. "It is though."

"Go out with me tonight."

My whole body literally jerks in shock that he has asked me that. His eyes are watching me intently. "Okay," I agree, and I start to freak out inside immediately.

I have never been on a date in my life. I've not prepared myself for this or asked Lani any questions.

He smiles for the first time. "After you." He puts his hand on the small of my back, leading me out.

I spot Lynn by herself and I walk over to her, trying to act cool and not freak out because I have a date.

She watches me as I walk to her. "Are you okay? I saw Lee run in after you, then Lane and Konrad," she questions, taking my hand.

"It was really weird. He wanted to speak to me but I told him no, that I was uncomfortable. He was standing outside of the bathroom when I opened the door." She looks over at Lee, who slips out of the gate. I hope he's leaving.

"What the fuck? He is so weird! I've noticed that he's creepy for a while now," she admits.

"Wait, you did too? I thought I was just paranoid," I confess, feeling more concerned now because I've caught him staring at her.

She nods, looking at the gate once again. "Yeah, I've seen him staring at you, but I've also caught him staring at Michaela more than once."

That pisses me right the fuck off. "I should have shot him." I'm half tempted to run after him after hearing about that. I am shaking mad. "Did Michaela notice?" I ask.

Lynn looks at the ground for a second. "She's the one who mentioned it to me."

That is the final straw for me. I leave Lynn standing and run out of the gate toward him.

I spot him immediately standing beside a car. "Hey," I call, walking up to him.

I can tell that I've taken him completely off-guard with my actions. It's one thing to fuck with me, but my niece? I will destroy you.

"I want to know what your problem is," I demand, my hands fisted at my sides so I don't knock him out.

His expression changes to one of anger. "You. I've tried to talk to you for months. I realize now you're a stuck-up bitch and a whore clinging to those men out there," he spits at me.

I laugh, shaking with the anger building up inside of me. "Look, say whatever you want about me, but I'm warning you, I catch you staring at my sister or my niece again, I will fucking end you. And I mean that with every part of my being."

He takes a step back at my threat. "I haven't..." he starts, but I throw my hand up.

"I don't give a flying fuck what you think you did, my niece was made uncomfortable by a grown-ass man. That is the issue. She brought it to her mother's attention! That is the problem and you made my sister along with my myself uncomfortable." I have my gun in the back of my pants and

I'm not afraid to use it. Honestly, I wish a motherfucker would.

His face drops. "Listen here, bitch. You do not speak to me like that! It's not your place!" he yells back, and it's like I've been hit by a ton of bricks. I am fucking floored by his words.

It sounds like the...

Konrad

Lynn runs to me, frantic. "Etta just ran after Lee. I let it slip to her that he made Michaela uncomfortable!" I take off running through the gates, pissed off at myself that I didn't even see her leave.

I spot her and him across the gravel yard. "Listen here, bitch!" I hear him yell, and I'm instantly enraged at the disrespect.

He lifts his hand like he's going to strike her. I grip her by the back of her shirt, pulling her back and behind me.

It happens so fast that he can't stop his movement, and he hits me in the chest instead.

His eyes widen as he takes me in; I can see the fear in his eyes. Lifting my hand, I take ahold of his fist. "Biiig fucking mistake," I chuckle, twisting his wrist with all of my strength, loving the fucking sound of the breaking of his bones.

"Please let me go," he pleads, his knees on the ground.

I tighten my hand on his wrist. "Please let me go," I mock his pathetic fucking voice. "I won't let you fucking go. You DARED to hit her!" I roar in his face, loving the way he flinches.

"I think he's from the cult," Etta whispers softly behind me. I look at her and her face is completely, utterly fucking pale. "He said, it's not my place." She's shaking.

FUCK.

I take out my phone and text Lane to get here ASAP. I don't

know her story, but I know that she grew up in a cult and they were fucked in the head.

Lee starts screaming, trying to pull away. "Get the fuck down!" I growl, pushing him down until his face is on the gravel, lifting his arm up higher so he can't move unless he wants to break his shoulder.

"Etta, look at me."

She looks at me, her beautiful eyes wide. "You're safe. No one can hurt you," I reassure her. I know that she's feeling some old shit right now.

She takes a deep breath, nodding. "Tell me who the fuck you work for," she demands, putting her foot on Lee's neck, pushing down.

Holy fuck.

He struggles to get away from her. "You will tell me or I'll shoot your fucking dick off. You have no other choices. Know your place, fucker." She throws his words right back at him.

I can't resist the urge to laugh. She's fucking hot. "Darlin', if you're trying to make me fall in love, it's working." I wink at her.

She grins, the light back in her eyes giving me exactly what I was hoping for.

"You're crazy," she tells me, laughing slightly.

I laugh right with her. "I don't think I'm the only one."

She shakes her head, turning the attention back to Lee. "Tell me the name of the fucking cult now!"

"Danielson!" he screams.

She takes a step back like he burned her, just as Trey runs up with her brother Vinny, Lynn, and my MC brothers. Vinny stops in his tracks at the word *Danielson*.

"This fucker tried to hit her," I tell them all. I'm still so fucking pissed. I want to put a bullet in his head. I want to end him for daring to hurt her.

"Danielson is the cult that we grew up in," Lynn tells everyone around us, letting it sink in.

He is there for them.

Etta

WHEN HE SPOKE THOSE WORDS, I knew. I knew because I heard them almost every single day of my life.

Know your place.

We were taught that we were nothing, that was all we would ever be in their eyes.

Lynn takes my hand. I know she's scared and, honestly, I am too. "Why are you here after so many years?" Lynn asks. Vinny wraps his arms around her tightly.

"You took my fiancée."

I blink and the silence around us grows as we each try to figure out who the fuck his fiancée could be.

Lynn pales to the point that I'm terrified she's going to pass out. "No!" she screams and then it hits me.

Michaela.

Fear unlike anything I have ever felt before overwhelms me. It's all-consuming. I take off running. I need to get to her. I can hear the others on my ass; I can't even feel my feet hitting the ground.

After running inside of the gate to the backyard, I stop for a second, trying to find Michaela, my heart beating so hard.

I don't see her, nor do I see Lani.

"Where is Lani!" Trey yells so loudly, I can hear the slight panic in his voice. Opening the door to the house, Konrad puts his hand on my back as we run through the rooms trying to find Michaela.

Looking out of the window to the front of the house, I see Lani holding onto Michaela, who is getting dragged by the father of the kid in Caleb's class. They're halfway across the huge-ass field where the parking lot is.

Oh my God!

Michaela is screaming at the top of her lungs. I rip open the door, and Konrad lifts me out of the way of Trey who runs past me.

A motorcycle comes to a stop across the field. Tristan gets off of his bike, coming to the party. "Tristan, help!" I scream at the top of my lungs. His head whips in our direction and takes in the scene; he is the closest to them.

I take off running behind Trey. Lynn passes me the fear for her child, spurring me to move faster. Everyone pushes past me as Lynn tries to get to Michaela and Lani.

Tristan rips the guy off of Michaela and starts beating the shit out of him right in front of everyone.

Lynn falls to the ground by her daughter, her legs not holding her up anymore. Trey picks up Lani, holding her, and Vinny is holding their kids.

I can't breathe with the terror I'm feeling. I would die if they had taken her. I would have murdered everyone in my path.

"Look at me." Konrad stands in front of me, cupping my face. "Breathe for me. She is safe," he repeats over and over until I finally connect the words he's saying.

"Oh my God, my baby," Lynn whispers over and over, holding onto Michaela, who is frozen in fear.

"Thank you," I tell Konrad, squeezing his hands on my face. I walk over to Tristan. He goes on every mission with me whenever he's home.

He's a Navy SEAL, and this was his last mission in the military before he retired. Now he's home for good. His eyes are glued on my sister and my niece. "Thank you for saving my niece." I don't bother to hide my emotions.

He gives me a hug. "I'm so fucking thankful. I just got back from my last mission."

Lynn looks up at him. "Thank you so much." Her eyes fill with tears as she rocks her daughter.

Tristan puts his hand on his chest, taking a step back. Lynn doesn't notice, all of her focus on Michaela.

"I need to get her home." Lynn stands up, struggling to carry her daughter.

"I'll take you home," Tristan volunteers. "Can I carry her for you?"

Michaela looks at Tristan before she nods. He lifts her and she cuddles into his chest. "Lynn, we will fix this shit," Trey tells her and Lynn nods, fire in her eyes.

We will not rest until every single person involved in this is dead, but that will never ever be enough.

They will suffer for this.

Etta

I HELP Tristan get Michaela into the car. She's in total shock, but I know without a doubt that she will pull completely through this.

Lani saved her life. Lani held onto her and didn't let go. That fucker hit her, kicked her, and tried his best to dislodge her so he could run.

"Wait, what happened to the little boy with them?" I ask Lynn. She looks around and shrugs. "I didn't see him with any of them."

Konrad says, "I'll go find him." He takes off running to the backyard, where everyone has left but the MC.

"I'm going to take them home," Tristan tells me, taking Lynn's hand and helping her inside the passenger seat.

Lynn looks down at his hand holding hers but does as he asks. I know she just wants to climb into bed with Michaela and never let go.

KONRAD

I'm emotionally exhausted too. First thing is that Lee got away. When everyone went to find Michaela, he slipped loose.

But we have the person that tried to kidnap Michaela. He is in such deep shit because he hurt an ole lady to the club and tried to kidnap one of the princesses. She may just be Vinny's niece but everyone loves her.

I can see Lani inside of the house, her guys and kids surrounding her as Myra the club doctor checks her over. Myra's coming to Lynn's next to check out Michaela.

Trey leaves the house and walks toward me. "Etta, you're going to go have to go under protection for a while; nowhere by yourself for a while until this shit is settled."

I knew this was going to happen. "I understand, Trey."

He looks inside Lynn's car as Tristan backs out. "Are you okay? This shit is so fucked up."

We have had peace in the MC for six years, then all of this happened at once on his kid's birthday party. It's beyond fucked up.

Trey runs his hand through his short hair. "I'll put a prospect on you tonight, unless you want to come live with us for a while?" he asks.

Konrad walks up, catching the end part of the conversation. "I have her tonight, brother."

My eyes go to Robert, the crying boy resting on his hip. "They were going to leave their baby? What the fuck is this?" Rage fills me to my core.

Trey closes his eyes, just now realizing. "I'll take him to the compound until we find information on him. We have plenty of mothers around to care for him."

My heart breaks at his tear-stricken face. I can tell he's so scared. "Hey there, sweetheart. Ready to go get some food and a warm bed?" I ask him in a soft voice.

He nods, but he doesn't move to leave Konrad. He just tightens his fist on his shoulder, which causes Konrad to grin.

I don't want to go there and admit how great he looks with a kid. "You don't have to babysit me." I don't want him to feel obliged.

His face hardens, that beautiful smile gone. "Being around you, I wouldn't call that fucking babysitting." He winks.

Lord bless my heart.

Trey is glaring at Konrad for flirting with me. "Follow behind me?" I ask Konrad.

He waves me forward. "Wouldn't want to do anything else," he flirts once again. My face burns with the attention of him doing this in front of Trey.

Vinny is my brother, but Trey? He's like my father. He has taken over the role and I am so thankful for him and everything he has done for me.

"Text me when you're home, Etta. Wear your earring, okay?" he tells me.

I was given a special earring years ago. It has a tracking device in it. If you're kidnapped, your abductors would never expect an earring to have a tracking device in it.

"I will."

I'm sure some would feel smothered, but I'd rather be safe and feel smothered than face the opposite.

"I'll follow behind you."

I look at Robert. "You okay, honey?" I ask. He must be so confused.

"What happened to Henry and Lee?" His little voice trembles. I am so mad. I am so mad that this happened and that this little boy has to suffer his consequences of their actions.

"Your dad is busy right now, sweetheart." I open the back door, hating that I don't have a booster seat for him.

"Henry is not my dad," he says as I buckle him. I look at Konrad, wondering if he's thinking the same thing I am. I smile at Robert. "Do you know where your momma is?"

His face falls. "She was bad and I'm not allowed to see her."

Fuck! I know exactly what has happened to her. He's been taken from his mother because they think she did something wrong and she's being punished for it.

"Sweetheart, what's your mom's name?"

He wipes his tears. "Maci."

I shut the door. "We need to find his mother."

Konrad opens my door for me, taking my hand and helping me inside. "Belt up, sweetheart."

I smile at the endearment and do as he asks. "Be careful, I will be right behind you." He shuts my door and walks over to a beautiful Harley.

Then it hits me that he's coming to the compound where I live. Nerves wrack me immediately, but that can't stop the excitement I feel on top of that.

3

ETTA

I CAN BARELY KEEP my eyes off of the mirror. Konrad looks way too good driving behind me, and I can't stop the thrill at the fact that he's following me.

My phone rings, and I'm so lost in my thoughts that it scares me for a second. It's from a number I don't know.

"Hello?"

"Hey, sweetheart. I'm going to have the prospect bring us some takeout for dinner. What do you want?"

Holy shit, I guess the date is still on?

I panic, not knowing what to say. "I like all food, just whatever you want."

He chuckles. "I'll just tell him to pick up random shit. See you in a bit, darlin'." He hangs up before I can say anything back.

Those damn butterflies are making themselves known in my stomach. He is so gorgeous and intimidating.

The drive back to the compound is way too short because I'm internally freaking out, but I'm also saddened by Robert quietly sniffling in the back.

His whole entire world has been flipped upside down. I want

to tell him so bad that I'm going to find his mother, but the disappointment isn't worth it if I can't.

I'll have to talk to Techy later to give him the information on Robert's mother. I know right now that Henry is in the pit and he is going through some kind of hell and that's something I will never regret.

I've never been in the pit, but I know that the guys dish out their own kind of justice down there and I don't have any ounce of sympathy for those who have been there.

Including my own father. He was so horrible to me and Lynn, but it was nothing compared to Vinny and Danny's experience. That was a different kind of hell.

The things done to me do haunt me, I feel those wounds, but it's nothing compared to knowing what happened to my siblings.

That is a whole different kind of hurt. My mother is out there somewhere and I do feel sorry for her because she was forced into that life also, but she allowed everything to happen. That is hard to forget.

I pull to a stop outside of the main house where I live, and before I can put the car in park, Konrad opens my car door.

"Thank you!" I say, putting my hand in his so he can help me out.

Looking at Konrad, you'd never think that he was such a gentleman. I open the back door. "Come on, little man." Konrad unbuckles Robert and lifts him out.

"How do you feel about a burger?" Konrad asks him, taking his hand. He's holding mine in one hand, the other holding Robert's.

Robert smiles. "A burger for me?!" He gets so excited and my heart melts at the precious little boy.

Inside the house, I spot Rosa, one of my main helpers. "I need you to find him a room to stay in and I need someone to watch him."

She waves her hand forward for Robert and he leaves with her. I text Techy the information about his mother. Honestly, I would be surprised if he doesn't already know about her; he has done a lot of research on our cult.

One thing about it is, it's *huge*. It spreads out all the way across the USA and it's growing daily.

"Are you okay?" Konrad asks when I put my phone back into my pocket. I push my hair out of my face and behind my shoulders.

"I'm exhausted. So much has happened today, it's catching up with me," I confess.

"Darlin', I can see that written all over your beautiful face. You were so brave today protecting your family." He cups my face slightly, his thumb brushing my cheekbone.

I hold my breath, the feeling of him touching me overwhelming. I'm not used to that.

My face burns from his touches. I know he can feel it. The doorbell rings and I look over to see a younger guy holding a huge bag. "Takeout is here." Konrad walks to the door, takes the food and shuts the door, locking it behind him.

"Where do you want to eat?" he asks.

"Do you mind if we go to the apartment upstairs?" I ask, but kind of regret it because it's my home, it's my personal space, but I just need to be in my own space where I feel safe.

He studies me for a few seconds, looking to see if I have any second thoughts. "Show me the way."

I lead him up the stairs to the main floor of the house. I unlock the door and push it open. "This is home."

He walks in studying everything. He sets the bag onto the counter. "So I had him pick up burgers, some pizza, Chinese, and other random things."

Here I am freaking out about him being in my space and what he thinks, but all he's worried about is food.

"I'm going to take one of the burgers down for Robert, then

KONRAD

I'll be right back." He squeezes my hand for a second before he slips out the door.

The second he leaves I let out a deep breath. I can't help but be on edge. I'm used to being around men all of the time, but this is different.

He's making me have feelings I've never experienced before. He makes me nervous and so happy at the same time. I need to wrap my head around it.

No matter how nervous I am, I want him here. I want to experience this. Without a doubt I feel safe with him.

I just need to get my heart to calm down to catch up with my head.

Breathe in, breathe out, I tell myself over and over until I'm better, my breathing back to normal and my heart slowing down.

I walk over to the bag of food and get everything out, along with some plates, some beers, and soft drinks.

"Want me to pay you back?" I ask once Konrad comes back.

He gives me a look. "Thanks for the offer, but if you're with me I pay for everything."

I huff at him being an alpha. He sets the plate down, giving me a look. "What was that, darlin'?" he asks.

I laugh, giving him back the same look. I reach behind me and take out my gun, placing it on the counter. "Wasn't a damn thing."

He bursts out laughing, holding his stomach. "Damn, better not fuck with you, huh?"

I wink. "Now you're getting it"

He licks his lips, moving closer to me until he's practically touching me with his whole body. "Good thing I love danger," he whispers into my ear, his breath tickling the side of my neck, chilling me down to my very core.

The person who is dangerous here is him.

He doesn't move, just lifts his hand above my head, taking

out a glass. His eyes stare deep into mine. I swear he can feel my heart beating so hard.

His eyes move to my mouth, then back up to my eyes. Is he going to kiss me? I lift my hand and press it against his side. I can feel the muscle beneath my hand.

"You're so fucking stunning. I can get lost in you," he tells me, his voice husky.

He steps back, leaving me breathless, then he gathers all of the food and takes it into my little living room.

I pick up my beer, taking a long pull, trying to ease my nerves. He sits down onto the couch and I sit down beside him, grabbing the remote and turning on the TV to fill the room with noise.

Konrad

She sits next to me, and I try to not look at her shaking hands. She is so fucking brave, the way she protected her family today. I was in awe of her.

But one thing I know is, she needs someone to protect her with the same ferocity that she protects everyone else.

She did not hesitate to protect her niece, nor did she hesitate to take Robert under her wing and bring him here.

I can see how fucking independent she is, the way she's used to doing everything for everyone, saving them and taking care of them.

She deserves that same kind of shit, I want her to feel safe with me, I want to know what put that fear in her eyes. I have caught that darkness at random times today and I will not forget the look on her face when they mentioned the cult.

"Do you like true crime?" she asks, breaking me from my thoughts.

I smile. "Yeah, I thrive on that shit."

She rolls her eyes, giving me attitude. "Yeah well, let's watch this documentary about this serial killer." She raises the remote to turn on the tv, before she stops looking at me. "If you want to."

"I don't give a fuck what we watch. I doubt I'll be staring at the TV much anyway," I flirt, and her face changes so much in a split second before she realizes I'm flirting with her.

I don't dare look away, loving every single second of her face changing so many different shades of red.

"You're staring at me," she mumbles before taking a bite of fries.

I look down at my plate, smiling. "I told you, the movie is not what I'll be staring at."

She shakes her head, grinning ear to ear. "You're not so bad-looking yourself," she tells me, looking me up and down.

I harden at the look she's giving me. "Darlin', you look like an angel compared to the way I look."

Etta

I AM the opposite of him. I'm all blonde hair, blue eyes and he is just completely covered in tattoos, which I think is very attractive.

"Looks are only skin deep. The nicest-looking men can be the worst," I point out, speaking from experience.

The men in our cult are clean-cut and always dressed nice, but look what kind of men they are—the worst that humanity can bring.

"You're right," he agrees with me.

"Do you have any siblings?" I ask.

"I was an only child; both of my parents are still together. You have Vinny, Lynn, and Danny. I've met all three, but I never met you until today."

Honestly it is kind of weird that we never met until today as he met everyone else in my family. "Kind of weird, isn't it?" I point out.

He nods. "Every time it was my time for a mission, my mom or dad seemed to get sick so I had to rush off to see them."

My heart aches. I'm sure it's hard your parents being sick. "Oh no, are they okay now?" I ask.

I can see the pain on his face at the mention of his parents. "They're older. Time is the worst fucking enemy you can have, isn't it?" I can almost feel the pain.

I can't resist the urge to reach over and squeeze his hand. "I am so sorry. If you need to go to them, I really understand. I'll be fine here."

I hate the idea that I'm keeping him away from his parents who need him. His face softens in a way I have never seen before.

"Darlin', just you offering means a lot to me. The nurse is there right now, so now I'm all yours." He winks as he says the last part.

I snort. "You're just a big flirt, aren't you?"

He shrugs his shoulders. "Darlin', it seems that you bring out the worst in me."

Lord, I wonder what the best of him is, and why do I have a feeling that he is really great at it?

I look away, afraid that I could give away my thoughts.

He doesn't let go of my hand, rather he holds on tighter, intertwining our fingers together.

"How about you slide that ass over here so I can cuddle you like a sappy fucker?" he asks bluntly.

Oh God, my body is screaming because I'm going to be so close to him, pressed against him, but I don't hesitate.

I scoot against him. He lets go of my hand and wraps his arm around my shoulder, pulling me to him.

Next my blanket is thrown across my lap. He wraps it around me, making sure I'm warm.

I'm stiffer than a board and I don't know what I should be doing. Do I lay my head on his chest?

I am twenty-four years old, I had never held a man's hand before until today and this is the first time I have cuddled someone.

He slowly glides his hand up my arm until he cups the side of my face, gently laying my head on his chest, and with his other hand he brings my left arm across his stomach, totally taking control.

I am completely, totally pressed against him and it's the best thing I have ever felt in my life.

Honestly, this is so small, but before this my PTSD stopped me from being in the same room as a man. They terrified me.

But now I feel safe, completely safe, and that is a rarity for me. I scoot even closer, bringing my head right under his chin, and he does the best thing ever.

He wraps both arms around me tightly, holding me to him. His arms are like steel, daring something to tear me away from him.

I want to say so much, I want him to know how huge of a deal this is and he just broke down some walls of mine.

I just stay quiet, enjoying this moment. The sound of the TV in the background and the feeling of being warm and safe lure me to sleep in minutes.

4

ETTA

My phone wakes me up. I jump and reach for it on the coffee table, taking in the room for a second before I answer.

Konrad is sitting up. We both fell asleep on the couch and the wall clock shows that it's three a.m.

"Hello?" I answer, my voice deep with sleep.

"Hi, is this Etta?" a young girl asks, and I sit up straighter. I know immediately she needs help.

"Yes, this is her."

I put it on speaker phone, setting the phone onto the counter so I can write down information.

She sniffs loudly and I can hear the sound of her chattering teeth. "Can you please help me? I was walking home. I snuck out of my house and these men picked me up off the side of the road. I can't get ahold of my parents and they are trying to find me."

"Where are you?" I ask, jotting down everything. We usually deal with cults, but I will do whatever it takes to help someone.

"I am right outside of Stevenson, outside of Raleigh."

"Send me your location. I'll be there ASAP."

A minute later, I get a ding and it lets me know that she's twenty minutes from here.

"I'm going to let you go, sweetie, but I am going to text you. I'm coming." I run into my closet and put on my gear, then throw Konrad a vest that I have spare for Vinny. "Ready for your first mission?" I ask him.

He gives me a wicked grin. "More than fucking ready."

We leave out of the back entrance to the house. I throw Konrad the keys to the SUV and run into the passenger seat. I put my AK on the floor, loading it and putting the strap around my shoulder.

Konrad keeps looking over at me. "This is the hottest fucking thing I have ever seen." I laugh and load his gun too, ready for him.

We go way over the speed limit and we make it to a wooded area in half of the time. I can see lights shining through the woods, men talking and I know they're searching for her.

Fuck me.

"Let's blow some fuckers up." I step out. "Shine your lights in the woods, let them know we're here."

Konrad looks at me with big eyes like I'm the best thing since sliced bread. He does as I ask and gets out to stand next to me. "I would fucking tell you to stay in the SUV, but I know you won't do that shit, but I ask you to stand behind me please? For my fucking sanity?"

I roll my eyes. "Since you asked nicely." I put my hand on his back. "Let's do this shit."

We look through our scopes so we can see in the dark, we can see their heat signatures. "I see something!" one of the men yells and I can hear twigs snapping as they rush in our direction. It means they aren't searching for her.

They rush out of the woods, right at the forest line. Their eyes are huge as they take us in, confused as to what is happening.

The men are not professional, I can tell you that right off the bat. They are dressed in baggy jeans, their shirts are disgusting, covered in food and filth. They are majorly skinny. I can see the darkness around their eyes, giving me a hint they are on drugs.

"Onto the fucking ground or I will use lethal force!" Konrad yells in a deep, scary tone and it's the best thing I have ever fucking heard.

They look at each other, unsure of what is happening. "Who the fuck are you guys?"

Konrad grins. I shiver at the sinister sight. This is not the same smile he has been giving me. No, this one is filled with darkness, pain, and the hell he has planned for these guys.

"Your worst fucking nightmare." I can feel my phone buzzing in my pocket. I sent the alert to the guys and let them know what was happening. We will have backup soon.

Oh shit, his voice, the absolute terrified look on their faces. I stroll forward from behind Konrad. "Boys, on your knees now." I flick my gun, pointing at the ground. "Or I can fucking end it now."

Konrad nods his head back, motioning for me to step behind him. I sigh and do as he asks, not wanting to distract him.

"Look, man, we're just playing hide and go seek here in the woods," the one on the right argues.

I laugh. "Do you think we found you for nothing? We know why you're out here. Do as he asks and we may let you live." I grin, loving the looks on their faces knowing they're caught.

One by one they get to their knees, but I know the one on the end is going to give us trouble when he looks to us and to the woods.

He takes off running, slipping off into the woods. "Fuck." I turn on my night vision scope. I can see him running through the woods on the thermal. I look around the woods until I see a small figure in the opposite direction he is running.

"Let's get these fuckers tied up and I'll go find him." Konrad walks over to the scum lying on the ground.

"Who are you guys?" one of them whispers, staring at Konrad fearfully.

I can't blame them for being scared, with the way he is dressed in his gear right now, and he is huge, tattooed everywhere. He is definitely intimidating.

"I am a member of the Grim Sinners MC, an Original." Konrad looks down at him pointedly. "Who the fuck are you?"

Why is he so attractive right now?

The guy's face pales further. "I'm sorry." He looks at the ground. I gather my zip ties, tying his legs and hands together so he can't get up.

"Why did you do it?" I ask. I want to know why someone would do this.

One of the guys next to him looks up at me as I tie his hands behind his back. Konrad is carefully watching to make sure they don't move.

"She turned down the guy who ran into the woods. We were meant to mess with her a bit but he took it too far."

I sigh. Men and their egos. We are not going to kill them, but we are going to dump them in the jail and we will give her family a lawyer to make sure they're sentenced to the fullest extent.

I look into the scope. I can see him still running and the girl is still in her same spot lying on the ground.

"I'm going to find him. Do you want to go to her?" Konrad asks.

I nod. "Yeah, that's a good idea. See you in a bit?" I ask, smiling.

He shakes his head, smiling. "Darlin', I'm in so much trouble when it comes to you. You will for sure see me in a bit and there better not be a scratch on your ass either."

"Or what?" I ask, arching an eyebrow, and then internally panic on the inside. Why did I say that?

I take off running into the woods. I peek back at him once again and I see him standing there staring at me.

I think I'm the one who's in trouble here.

I turn on my flashlight and follow the thermal to the girl. I call her before I reach her. "Hey, it's me," I tell her once I hear her breathing over the phone. She probably thought I was one of the guys.

I hear her breath hitch as she sobs into the phone. I shine my light in her direction, and she slides out from under a bush. Her face comes into view and my heart breaks a little. She doesn't look like she's older than fourteen or fifteen years old.

"Etta?" she asks, her voice trembling.

"That's me. We caught the guys. One ran off but I have someone tracking him now." I grab her hand and she clings to me.

"I am so sorry I snuck out of the house. I just wanted to walk to the lake and read," she sobs. My heart hurts because of this small mistake. It cost her a lot.

This is going to affect her whole life. She's going to be jaded and fearful, but I'm so thankful that I got here in time. No matter what those guys say, they went along with it.

"Sweetheart, what is important is that you're safe."

Her phone starts going off and she looks down at the screen. "It's my dad."

"Do you want me to talk to him?" I ask her.

She nods, laying her head on my shoulder as we stand in the middle of the woods. "Hello," I answer.

"Who is this? Where is my daughter Gabby?" he yells into the phone. I know he is terrified.

"Sir, I am with the Hope House." I explain what happened, what she told me. "She is safe, I will bring her home."

"No, I will come to you now. I need to see my baby." I can hear a woman in hysterics through the phone as the dad speaks.

I hang up the phone, not wanting to be distracted a second longer. The other guy is still out there.

I raise my scope and look through it. I see Konrad right on his ass, but the bad part is...

He's running straight for us.

I can see the light in the distance.

"Come, we need to go." I take Gabby's hand and run through the woods, looking back at the light to make sure we're getting away from him.

One second the light is there, the next it's gone and I hear a blood-curdling scream.

Gabby clutches me, her nails digging into my shirt as she holds my arm tightly. "What was that?" she whispers in horror.

I smile when I hear another horrific sound. "The person with me just found the last guy."

She lets out a deep breath. I can tell she's relieved. Looking through my scope confirms what I thought—Konrad is beating the shit out of him.

I laugh, putting my gun down, and we trek through the woods. I can hear motorcycles in the distance.

"What is that sound?" Gabby asks. She is so incredibly pale.

"Reinforcements. You are safe. Your parents are on their way," I reassure her. She nods and practically lies on top of me as I walk her out of the woods.

The first step out of the woods, I see Smiley running in our direction, I guess to come find us. Lane is watching the men we tied up.

"Where is Konrad?" Maverick asks, running up, the whole entourage popping up.

"He went to find the last guy. Apparently he was the one who planned this." I give him the information that we know.

Maverick looks at Gabby, his face soft. "I'm sorry, sweetheart, are you okay?" he asks.

She nods. "I'm so glad you found me. The things he planned to do... I could hear them talking inside the car. I pulled the latch inside of the car and jumped out once they slowed down," she rushes out more information.

I look at the guys and see they are trying to conceal their anger. "Come on, sweetheart." I lead her to my SUV and open the back so she can sit inside. I grab a blanket and wrap it around her shoulders.

She shivers, pulling the blanket tighter around her. "I can feel them watching me."

I look over to the group of guys lying on the ground. They are staring at her. "Smiley, those fuckers are making her uncomfortable."

He turns them onto their backs so they're staring at the sky. "I feel so stupid that I snuck out of the house."

I run my hand down the back of her hair, pulling out some leaves as I go. "Sweetheart, I think blaming yourself is an unnecessary punishment. You have learned a horrible, hard lesson. I think that's enough."

Self-blaming hate is the worst. It can eat you alive. I don't want that for her. She is so young.

She nods, and then a large truck pulls up in front of us. I step in front of her, ready to protect her. "That's my dad," she whispers.

He jumps out of the truck with her mother on his heels. "Daddy," she sobs, and I couldn't stop the tears if I tried. He picks her up, holding her against him tightly. "My baby, I am so sorry," he tells her over and over.

Someone walks up to the side of the SUV. I turn around and see Konrad walking to me. "Took you long enough," I tease.

He laughs. "Had to have a little fun first."

I grin at that. "I saw it through the thermal," I confess. He puts his hand on my back and we watch the touching moment between father and daughter together.

I am relieved to know that her home life seems to be good. It was just a stupid, horrible mistake and it cost her a lot.

Her dad finally looks at me. "Are you the girl I talked to?" he asks.

"I am Etta. I run Hope House. I do this kind of thing almost daily."

He closes his eyes. "I am thankful for what you have done. Where are the fuckers?" I can see the change in him before my eyes.

I look over at the guys lying on the ground. "We are going to take them to the jail, but I won't say a word if you want a few minutes alone with them."

Konrad chuckles. "I already messed one of them up, but there's room for improvement."

The dad grins at that. "Show me the way." Konrad leads him down the slight hill.

"Why don't you guys join me over here?" I don't want Gabby to see this.

We all stare into the darkness, trying to ignore the sounds of people getting their asses beat behind us.

She laughs randomly, covering her mouth to stop herself. "I shouldn't be laughing, but I feel like I'm getting justice a little, right?" she says.

"You sure are, honey." Her mom rubs her back. I can see that haunted look on her face.

"My sister is a therapist. She's an expert in this kind of thing. She can help adjust to life again, if you're interested?" I ask her.

Her mom nods immediately. "That would be so amazing. Does she have a card?" I walk to the front to get a card.

I look over at the guys. The dad is stomping someone's face currently. That had to hurt.

I text the guy at the jail, letting him know we are coming in.

I give him brief details so he has an idea of how many and what happened. The prospects will handle the rest.

Konrad walks over to me. "You feeling okay?" he asks, touching my arm gently to get my attention.

I give him a confused look. "Yeah, I'm fine."

He smiles. "Good, they're loading them and then we can head back."

I am exhausted. "I think I could sleep for a full day. I need to give the mom Lynn's card."

I walk over to the mom. "Here is her card. We have our own lawyer, unless you have your own."

She smiles at me for the first time. "I am a lawyer, darlin'. We got this covered from here." She takes the card and hugs her daughter tight. "Her dad owns a boxing gym here in town."

I look over and see that huge-ass fist. "Yeah, I think he's getting tons of practice in right now," I joke, lightening the mood.

They both bust out laughing. "I needed that, thank you."

Their eyes turn to look behind me. I look around and see the dad is coming back. "Ready to go home?" he asks.

They nod. The girl hands me the blanket back and her dad tucks her into his side. "Thank you, Etta, you saved my life," she whispers, her eyes filling with tears again as she thinks of what could have happened.

"Anytime, anywhere. If you need me, I'm there."

She nods once and is taken away by her parents. She will be okay. She's strong, she got away on her own.

"She will be fine." Konrad voices my thoughts.

"She will be," I agree.

The guys make their way over to us. The prospects are carrying the kidnappers into a van. "Get some sleep, thank you for coming to help." I thank the guys.

Smiley touches my shoulder. "I got your back always, honey." Then he gives Konrad a look.

Why do I feel like that had a double meaning??

I see all of the guys looking at Konrad funny, then it clicks. They're trying to be protective. "Aww, you guys." I move over and give them all a group hug. They all awkwardly pat me on the back.

We get back inside of the SUV, Konrad behind the wheel once more. "I wanted to check her to make sure she was not hurt, but I was afraid my presence would scare her."

I start to reach over and touch his hand instinctually but I stop myself. "She is in a very fragile state right now. Do you have medical experience?" I ask.

He smirks. "Darlin', I'm a doctor. I was one in the military for a long-ass time."

"Oh wow, I didn't know that. I could have used you sooner," I joke, and he laughs slightly.

"Use me anytime," he retorts, giving me a wink.

I am so in trouble. I look out of the window and try to hide my burning face.

Konrad

I grin to myself knowing she can't see me. She's looking out of the window, but I see the blush covering her face and neck.

She is fucking adorable.

I saw a side of her tonight that floored me. She is so fucking soft, but she goes into protector mode in a split second.

We arrive back to the compound. I pull back into the garage, then hurry around before she can get out so I can open her door for her.

She looks at me in surprise when I do that. I take her hand and she slides out of the SUV.

"Thank you." She smiles bashfully, looking at the ground. I don't let go of her hand as we walk back upstairs to her apartment at the top of the house.

I can't leave her considering the fucking cult was there for her niece and that means she's in danger by association.

If I'm being honest, I'm using it as an excuse. I don't want to leave her, plus the thought of someone hurting her really pisses me the fuck off.

She pushes open her door and unsnaps her vest, throwing it on the recliner before bringing her hands up to her bun, taking her hair down, her fingers rubbing her scalp.

Damn.

She turns around to look at me, her eyes widening like she forgot I was there. "I'm exhausted," she breathes, rubbing her eyes. "I'm going to go take a shower. Make yourself at home."

She practically runs off to the bathroom. I pull off my vest and plop it down next to hers.

Etta

I AM SCARED, terrified of this man. Not in a way where I am scared for my life, but I'm scared because he's making me feel things I've never felt before.

The way he was looking at me before I ran into the shower, it was a lot. I couldn't miss his desire for me, but he had so much more in his gaze than that.

I am scared of that.

I want to be a normal twenty-four-year-old having sex, meeting guys, and living the best life.

I'm scared. Sex has always had negative associations for me, and I still have that in my head sometimes, no matter how much therapy I undergo.

People claim that it's the best thing ever, but I can't help but feel that fear and doubt.

I know that's not happening tonight, but that is a fear of mine. It can't be helped. I can't help the thoughts I think or the feelings I feel.

Then it hits me that I didn't bring any clothes to change into. "Hey Konrad, can you bring me something to wear? Just open the door and drop it in?" I ask loudly so he can hear me.

A few minutes later the door opens just enough to slip something in. I can't help but smile at him being respectful and not taking a peek.

I knew he was gentleman, but this just made him ten times more attractive to me.

I turn off the shower, dry and lotion my body, brush my teeth and I gather the clothes he gave me.

I stare in shock at the shirt he gave me. It's his. I laugh and hesitate to put on his shirt. I take a deep breath, breathing in his smell before I slip it over my body and put on the boy short panties he dropped in too.

I won't be scared, not anymore. My abusers don't deserve to make me feel that way anymore. I am my own woman now.

I turn off the light and push open the door. Konrad is sitting on the edge of the bed looking through the TV channels.

He is shirtless and wearing a pair of jeans. My eyes go to his abs—he has an eight-pack at least. He has chest hair and it speckles all the way down to his happy trail.

He is the most beautiful man I have ever seen, hands down. I start to shake at the intensity of his gaze.

"Do you want some sweatpants or something?" I stammer out. He nods, his eyes not leaving me for a second, like he's trying to memorize everything.

He stands and I walk to my closet, getting the biggest pair of sweatpants I can find. He takes them from me, his hands settling on mine for a second, our eyes connected.

I slide onto the bed and pull the covers over my legs. He steps out of the closet and I almost fall over from laughing so hard.

The sweatpants are literal leggings on him. I snort and hold my stomach. He turns around, and I cover my mouth because his butt is absolutely huge. "I never knew men could have big butts like that," I tease.

He laughs with me. "I think I'll have to just sleep in my boxers."

I nod in agreement, tears rolling down my face, but that soon stops when I see him standing in front of me in just his boxers.

He walks over and turns off the lights and moves in the direction of the living room, sitting on the couch.

Instantly I'm disappointed. "The couch is very small. I have plenty of room here. If you wanted, just to sleep." I had to elaborate the last part, my face burning. *He probably didn't even know that, Etta!* I scold myself.

He hesitates before walking to me. "Darlin', the last thing I want to do is to make you uncomfortable or feel unsafe in your own home. I can sleep here just fine."

I don't think I could feel safer than I did earlier in his arms. "Come on, I feel safe with you."

I know what my words have done to him. His expression changes to one that has my heart skipping a little beat. He walks to me slowly, pulling back the blanket and lying next to me.

"Plus it's a little cold in here," I say nonchalantly.

"Yes, that's definitely it, darlin'." His eyes twinkle, showing his amusement. I turn on my side to face him, and I smile, studying his face.

He catches me looking and turns to face me just as I am here. "But for what it's worth, sweetheart, there's nowhere else I'd rather be than here." He lifts his hand, pushing my hair off of my face and over my shoulders, his hand coming around to cup the side of my neck.

"I want to kiss you," he states.

Butterflies take over my stomach. I shakily lift my hand to his on my neck. "What's stopping you?" I whisper, shocked I even said that but proud of myself.

He doesn't waste a second. He presses his lips to mine, completely taking over and kissing me until my toes curl.

Every single part of my body is tingling, desire pooling between my legs on top of shaking so hard I'm sure he is feeling it.

His finger strokes my cheekbone. He kisses me gently, tenderly, and it has so much feeling behind it.

This means something.

This is also my first true kiss, the one I wanted and not one where my ex just smashed his mouth to mine before he did what he wanted.

I move closer, putting my hand on his shoulder to anchor myself. His fingers drift from my face, burying in my hair, pulling me closer, controlling my movements.

He slowly pulls away, his eyes opening, looking into mine. He leans forward, kissing me gently on the forehead, placing a sweet, caring kiss there. "Goodnight, baby," he whispers.

My eyes fill with tears. That small kiss on my forehead was one of respect and tenderness.

I have never felt that before.

I scoot closer, throwing my leg over his, cuddling into his side, feeling so safe and warm. "Goodnight, Konrad."

5

ETTA

I WAKE up on my stomach with Konrad practically lying on top of me. I smile and pull the pillow under my neck, loving waking up like this.

His hand is rubbing my back, hip, and legs. "Good morning," he whispers in my ear, pushing my hair over my shoulder and kissing my cheek.

"Good morning." I look over and smile. His hair is mussed up on one side.

"I want to take you out for some late breakfast." He wraps his arm around me, hugging me further into his front.

I could lie here forever.

"Okay," I mumble, closing my eyes again for a second. He slides out of bed, taking all of the heat with him.

"It's cold." My teeth chatter.

He walks into my closet. I sit up and pull my legs to the side of the bed. He comes back a second later with a sweatshirt of mine and a pair of leggings.

Is he really going to dress me?

He stops in front of me. "Arms up," he tells me, and I lift my arms. He lifts his shirt over my head, and all I'm wearing is a sports bra.

What shocks me is he doesn't look down at me. He keeps his eyes on my face the whole time.

He truly respects me.

I put my arms through the holes, warming me instantly. "Is that better?" He takes a hold of my hand.

"Much." My voice is thick from emotions, ones I'm not used to feeling.

He bends over, putting my legs through the leggings and I stand up, his eyes on me once more as he lifts them up and over my butt, not once touching me in a sexual way.

It's like this is his way of letting me know that I can trust him.

My heart is heavy. "Sit back down, honey." I do as he asks. He grabs my hairbrush and a ponytail holder.

He moves behind me, his legs on either side of me. I close my eyes at the first feel of the brush bristles moving along my scalp and hair.

I sit here and let him brush my hair over and over, then he gathers my hair in the back, his fingers moving through the strands, then I hear the snap of the hair tie. I look over and see he has braided my hair down my back.

"Konrad, you make me feel cherished." My heart hurts from all of the emotions I'm feeling at once.

His face softens and his hand wraps around the bottom of my chin. "That's all I ever want from you, darlin'."

I can't resist the urge. I turn around and crawl up to him, wrapping my arms around his neck, needing to feel close to him.

He lifts me so my legs are on either side of him. His hands snake their way under my sweatshirt, running down my back.

There is a loud knock at the door and I jump completely off

his lap, holding my heart. I'm not used to others coming up here.

Konrad doesn't let me go far. "Hey, it's just a prospect bringing me clothes. Are you okay?" he asks.

I nod, laughing it off. "Yes, I'm fine, I just got startled."

He studies me a few seconds before he goes to the door. "Knock quieter next time, fucker." Konrad grabs his stuff and slams the door shut.

I laugh loudly. "You didn't have to do that."

He gives me a look. "I don't give a fuck. He scared you. I don't like that shit, ever."

There go those damn butterflies. He slips into the bathroom to get changed and I take my phone off of the nightstand, noticing I have a missed call from Techy.

I call him back. "Hey, what do you have for me?" I ask.

"Good news. I found Robert's mother. They have her in a house for the women they deem bad and need exorcized."

I jolt at the last part. Fear fills my stomach. That was what was about to happen to me. My family was the last resort before I was sent away there.

This is where they send the women who don't mind their husband. They claim the devil is inside of them and that they must exorcize the demon out.

It's hell. They starve you, hurt you, beat you, rape you, on top of the exorcism that you get daily.

Not many things scare me, but that absolutely terrifies me. "Oh God, Techy, this is really bad. We need to go tonight to get her out. This is extremely important. I hope she's still alive," I rush out and pace the room, my anxiety through the roof.

"We have to get all of the women out of there. This is going to be a big mission. I need to contact Kyle and Lane. These girls are being tortured."

He hangs up and I drop the phone onto the bed. I gather my

vest and gun off of the chair. We have a meeting room here, so we can formulate a plan when the guys arrive.

This is so, so bad.

Konrad has to come. I know without a doubt that these girls are going to need medical attention.

Konrad walks out of the bathroom. I'm borderline having a panic attack and I know once Lynn hears this, it's going to freak her out just as bad.

You think fearing your husband, your abusers is bad, but this? This is literal hell on earth. These women are not women in the cult's eyes, they are meant to be broken.

"Etta, what's wrong?" Konrad rushes to me and takes my face in his hands. "We found Robert's mom. It's so bad." I sob the last part.

His body stiffens before he pulls me to his chest, comforting me. "What's so bad, Etta?" he asks, his voice void of emotion.

I let out a deep breath, my voice cracking. I sit down onto the side of the bed and he sits next to me. I tell him exactly what happens there, what she is going through.

"I was almost sent there. They were coming in a matter of days before my brother took me out of that life."

Konrad looks at me in shock. "That almost happened to you?"

I nod. "I was forced to marry when I was fourteen years old. My husband, Kenneth, was a very horrible man and he was around thirty years old when I married him. Lynn was forced to marry at thirteen. She had a two-year-old by the time she was sixteen."

Konrad gives me the most heartbreaking look. "Baby," he whispers. He reaches to touch me but fists his hands together in anger. "Is he still alive?"

I look at him in confusion. "Who?"

"The fucking pedophile? Your husband." He spits out the last word.

I nod. "Yeah, he is. Vinny never found him."

Konrad smiles. It's scary. "He won't be for much longer."

Oh fuck.

"Almost everyone in the cult is abused, but they don't break the cycle. It's hell but it's nothing compared to what Robert's mom is going through." My hands are shaking at the thought.

Konrad pulls me into his arms, setting me on his lap. "Darlin', it fucking breaks my heart the shit you went through." He grips my face gently, looking me dead in the eye. "I will make a promise to you. I will fucking make him suffer and whoever dared to hurt you."

Oh fuck, I can see the sincerity behind his eyes. "You don't have to do that," I whisper.

He shakes his head. He is trembling with anger. "Darlin', it fucking kills me that someone even touched you in any way that hurt you. When I see you, I see someone who deserves to be fucking cherished, cared for."

My bottom lip trembles as I try to hold back the tears. I am overwhelmed with so much right now.

He pulls me into him and holds me so tight, like he's afraid I'm going to be taken away from him.

I feel so safe and vulnerable at the same time, my story is known, but speaking it to a guy that I like? It's so different and it's scary because you don't know how anyone is going to react.

"I feel safe with you," I whisper, lifting my head to look at him. His face shows his appreciation at my words.

"Darlin', you're safe with me, always." He kisses my forehead and lets out a deep breath, the silence surrounding us.

My stomach growls loudly, breaking the quiet. He laughs. "Come on, let me feed you." He lifts me onto the ground, taking my hand, and we walk down to where his motorcycle is parked.

He hands me a helmet. "Ready to ride?" he asks, his eyes firmly on me, watching my every move.

KONRAD

Why do I feel like he's asking me for more than that? I take the helmet, buckling it in. "More than ready."

He grins widely, sliding on first. I take his hand and slide in behind him. He brings his hands behind my calves, pulling me flush against his back, and my hands rest on his abs.

He takes off and I close my eyes. The air is slightly chilly. This is amazing and what I needed. I needed to get out of my head.

He drives through town to a new little restaurant. It's two o'clock in the afternoon but they serve breakfast all day long.

We are seated, and much to my surprise, Konrad sits next to me. "Are you coming on the mission tonight? Lane and Kyle will be at the compound later. We need to plan."

He flips the menu over. "Where you go, I go." He gives me a cheesy wink and I giggle.

"We need to bring the medical van—you're a doctor and all." I bump my shoulder into his arm.

He grips the menu hard. I wince internally because I brought up the bad shit again.

"Darlin', drop that fucking look. I was thinking of those women. It's not you," he reassures me, seeing my look.

I nod. "Bossy," I mutter under my breath loud enough for him to hear. He laughs and kisses my temple.

It takes me by surprise for a second. I'm not used to so much physical contact but I like it—and I like it a lot coming from Konrad.

The waiter takes our order. "For our second date I'll take you to a fancy restaurant."

This is a date? I can't stop the smile at the knowledge. "Okay." I smile at him, his eyes going to my dimples.

"Darlin', have I told you how fucking heartbreakingly beautiful you are?" he tells me bluntly, causing my poor heart to race once more.

"Konrad," I whisper and lay my head on his shoulder. "You're so kind to me."

He wraps his arm around me, cuddling me close right in the middle of the restaurant. "I want to do a lot of things to you."

Blink, blink. It takes me a few seconds to wrap my head around what he's saying and I bust out laughing.

He chuckles with me, tucking a strand of hair that's fallen from my braid behind my ear. He watches me laugh. I try to cover my mouth, but he tears my hand away. "Don't hide it."

"What?" I ask, wiping under my eyes from laughing so hard.

"Your smile, baby." I internally sigh. I'm not sure how to even react around him. I smile and look down at the menu, feeling lightweight and just so happy. This is all so new for me.

"I need to check on my sister and Michaela. Do you mind stopping off there before we head back to the compound?" I ask.

"Yeah, sure thing."

WHEN I GET to my sister's I knock on the door. Usually I just walk straight in but I don't want to scare Michaela.

I can see Lynn peering from the kitchen to see who it is. She smiles and walks to the door. She has her finger to her mouth to make sure I'm quiet.

I step inside of the house. I look into the living room to see Tristan holding Michaela, who is fast asleep. Tristan is out too.

Lynn waves me into the kitchen. I follow her, with Konrad right behind me. "How is she?' I ask.

Lynn sits down, holding her face. "She has a therapy session later with one of my good friends. She didn't sleep all night until she crawled into Tristan's lap." She stops, tears filling her eyes. "She's hurting. There's nothing I can do to help her. They almost got my baby. I'm not sure I can recover from that." Her voice cracks into a sob. I walk over and pull her to me, hugging her tight and letting her cry all of the tears she wants.

I look over at Konrad, who looks unsure of what to do, but the worst part of this is…there's nothing you can do.

Me and Lynn have suffered a lot in our lives, but we have protected Michaela from all of that. Our past life hasn't touched her.

Until now, her almost getting kidnapped and her being promised to someone was beyond the realms of possibility. I never dreamed that this would happen.

It kills me inside knowing the fear she had. He was someone that we knew and he was always around. There is that betrayal on top of that; she will look at people different now.

That's heartbreaking.

I do hope that she's young enough and that she will forget it, but I know Lynn will make sure she will get through this and I'll be right there with her.

"MOMMY!" Michaela screams at the top of her lungs.

Lynn jumps out of her seat and is through the door in a second. Michaela is sitting up looking around for Lynn.

She lets out a deep breath when she sees Lynn. "I'm here, baby, you okay?" she asks.

Michaela settles her head back on Tristan's chest. He tugs the blanket up and holds her tighter.

His jaw is clenched. I know he is beyond pissed. "I was scared you were taken. I'm going to go back to sleep now." She tucks her hand under her chin, her eyes closing.

Tristan puts his hand on the back of her head like she's a small child. Lynn sits down next to Tristan and she leans her head back against the back of the couch. I know she's exhausted.

"We're going to go. Call me with updates, please, or if you need me." I bend over and give her another hug, lingering a few extra seconds.

It's engrained in me to protect my sister and my niece. I have protected Lynn for as long as I can remember. I would get in trouble so the eyes would be off of her and on me.

Vinny did the same thing for Danny, Danny did the same for me, and I did it for Lynn. That's how we survived.

I shut the door gently behind me so I don't wake Michaela. I stare off into the field. "This breaks my heart," I tell Konrad.

He looks just as sad as I do. "Darlin', it's fucking heartbreaking, but she is strong, like her mom and her aunt." He takes my hand and tugs me to his chest, hugging me. "But let's go kick some ass." At his words, I grin ear to ear. "Let's."

Time to have some fun.

Etta

WE'RE GETTING GEARED up here at the compound; we are making a straight shot there.

The quietness surrounding us is astounding. We're all mentally preparing ourselves for what we are going to see.

I have heard rumors my whole life of what to expect, but I am deathly afraid to come face to face with it.

My fear is nothing compared to what those girls are suffering, what they have been through and are probably still going through.

I won't let the fear get to me; they deserve my strength.

Konrad tightens my bulletproof vest straps on my sides, making sure it's fastened securely.

The prospect is bringing the medical van for everyone who needs medical care. Konrad insists on driving me.

"Are you okay?" he asks, his eyes studying my face to make sure I'm not lying.

When I was telling the guys what that place is, they had to know what they could possibly come face to face with.

Vinny and Danny are coming also. They added onto what I told them, letting them know what they heard.

My brothers are riding with me. They want to be close after all of the shit has been happening.

I can't wrap my head around the fact that after all these years, they are still trying to fuck with our lives.

They have no regard for women and children. My brothers were being groomed to be the next generation of fucked up men, but they left. They broke the cycle.

I know I won't stop until all of these fuckers are dead, in hell, where they belong.

6

KONRAD

THE DRIVE there is fucking killing me. Etta is shaking in the seat next to me and that shit alone is fucking with my head.

I reach over and take ahold of her hand, fucking hating the feeling of her hand shaking in mine.

Vinny and Danny are looking out of the window deep in thought in the back seat.

What the fuck is going on here? What the fuck are we stepping into that has all three of them fucking terrified?

What has that haunted look on their faces? I know my brothers are feeling the exact same thing.

It's going to be fucking bad.

Etta

WE PULL over on the side of the road, out of the way, so we can sneak around the house.

We don't want to give them time to hurt the girls, try to kill them to silence them, use them as hostages.

"Etta." I look over to Konrad. He takes my hand and pulls me to the side away from everyone.

He lets out a deep breath. "Darlin', you don't have to be brave right now. Stay with me. I will keep you safe, but please don't force yourself. I know you're scared; it's okay to be scared, honey," he says, soft enough for only me to hear.

I close my eyes, his words affecting me right now. I was trying with every fiber of my being to be strong, be tough.

Dealing with other cults is one thing, but when it's the one you grow up in? It's different. PTSD is something I fight with.

"You'll be with me?" I repeat, being vulnerable.

His jaw clenches, and he cups my face softly, tenderly. "Darlin', I will protect you, always."

His words are like a balm. They soothe an achy part of my heart. He takes my hand and we walk together into the woods. My brothers are standing on my free side.

Lane and Kyle are walking in front of the group, leading everyone. Prospects are at the vans and we will call them when it's time for them to come pick up the girls.

The house comes into view. It's huge enough to fit quite a few people and right in the middle of the yard is a woman, naked, chained to a pole. I can see her moving.

"Fuck is that?" Lane asks.

"A woman," I answer. I pick up my gun, throwing the strap over my shoulder, my protective instincts kicking in.

I am ready to protect these women. I am ready to take them out of this fucked up life.

This is what I am meant to do. It's time to show this fucking cult that no matter how much they abuse us, women are unstoppable. We may bend, but we don't fucking break.

It's time to show them that years ago we fractured them, but this time? It's time to end it completely.

When they hear my name, I want them to shake in fear.

I look at Konrad, nodding, letting him know I'm good.

Lane raises his hand, motioning for some of the guys to run through the woods to the back of the house so no one escapes.

We all stand in wait, all of us watching the women roll on the ground trying to get comfortable. She tries to roll over but the way she is chained doesn't allow for that to happen.

Lane looks at his phone. "They're in place."

We all take off running. "Danny, unchain her!" I tell my brother. I don't want to leave her outside by herself.

She looks at us in horror. I'm sure it's a scary sight to see all of us running straight toward her.

We can't stop though. Danny splits off and goes to her, taking off his shirt so he can cover her.

Konrad puts his arm in front of me, stopping me as Kyle kicks in the door. We are hit with a sickening stench. The smell of feces and piss is overpowering.

As we step inside of the house, we see a woman is lying chained on top of a small coffee table, her head and her legs on the floor. The only thing supporting her is the small table in the middle. I know she is in agony.

"Fuck!" Wilder yells and runs over to help her.

We all split up. Me, Vinny, and Konrad run upstairs with some other guys with us. I stop in the first room I see, where there is cage after cage smashed together just big enough for someone small to sit inside.

The most horrific part—there are people inside.

The women are backed as far as they can go. "Who are you?" one of the women asks, her voice cracking.

"We are from Hope House. I am Etta. We are getting you out of here." I rein back my emotions.

That's when the bathroom door opens and a huge man steps into the room. Konrad lifts his gun, hitting him hard in the face and knocking him out. "We need to keep him alive," Konrad informs me.

KONRAD

I walk over to the cages and they all have locks on them. "Fuck, I need some cutters."

I look at the caged women. Their eyes are huge, their faces are hollow from not getting enough food and they're all naked. "I will be back. I'm going to locate all of the other girls," I let them know.

The one who spoke earlier says, "There are a few new girls under the house. The secret doorway is in the office behind the bookshelf."

I leave the light on. Konrad walks in front of me and I grip the back of his shirt so we stay close together.

I turn in to the next bedroom, where a woman is lying on the bed motionless, her eyes looking at us without any life.

The next room is filled with cages once more—woman after woman piled on top of each other.

We did not bring enough vans; this is more than I ever expected. "Konrad, this is so bad. We need to call in some reinforcements," I tell him.

He nods. "Let's go find Lane and Kyle."

We find them in one of the rooms upstairs trying to break open some of the cages. "We need more vans and medical. I think we need to call in the girls for extra help," I tell them.

"I was just thinking that, but I don't fucking understand why there is no one here but the one fucker you found?" Lane questions.

I shrug my shoulder, thinking the same thing. "One of the girls mentioned a basement." I look over at one of the girls in a cage beside us. I take the cutters off of the floor, tearing off the lock and pulling it open.

She slowly crawls out. I know her body is killing her from being in the same position for so long.

My heart breaks, knowing what happens here, but seeing it? They are in fucking cages for a dog the size of a golden retriever. They are starved and I can see how abused they are. They are forced to lie in their own shit and piss.

This is the worst thing I have ever seen in my life. I try to make myself numb to it.

Lane hands me a blanket and I wrap it around her. The woman closes her eyes at that. She slowly moves to the bed and sits on the edge. "Thank you. Are you here to move us?" she asks. She isn't looking at us.

"No, sweetheart, we are here from Hope House."

She gasps and looks at me. "Etta?" she questions.

I nod. "That's me."

She starts sobbing, clutching the blanket to her, and I don't know what to do. I'm scared to touch her.

"I tried to contact you and I got into trouble. That's how I got here. Most of the girls here are here for the very same thing."

I look at the guys, all of us hurt to our core that they wanted our help but this happened to them instead.

"You are going to get out of here. We're going to take care of you," I tell her softly.

She sniffs and I smile at her. "We need to tell the house mom to move everyone out of the main house so we can move these girls in," I tell one of the prospects who helps out at Hope House. He nods and walks out of the room to do just that.

Konrad takes the cutters. He moves into the next room and I join, with the blankets. Ten cages in the next room—*snap, snap, snap.* The wild eyes of the women inside show they're scared out of their minds.

"I am with Hope House. I am Etta." Once they hear my name they start sobbing. It hits me like a ton of bricks that my name gives them comfort. They know I am here for them and I will get them to safety.

"Thank you so much," one of the younger girls sobs. She's

around sixteen or seventeen. She moves to hug me, and Konrad reaches out, taking her hand. She gasps in pain.

She is missing two fingers. It looks like they were cut off and her hand is healing horribly. "Prospect, put her in the medical van. I need to get antibiotics in her, ASAP."

Her eyes tear at that. "Something for the pain too?" she asks so softly, afraid.

Konrad gently lets her hand go. "Yes, sweetheart."

She lets the prospect take her out.

"Fuck," he cusses. I'm shaking with anger myself.

We move to the next room. These have fucking cages stacked on top of each other. These are wooden cages with just one small hole to let in a small bit of light. "Fuck, please don't tell me there are people in there."

These cages are super small. You'd have to lie down to get inside and they are long. They look like coffins.

Konrad puts his hand on my shoulder, halting me. "I'll do it." He walks over and cuts off the lock, opening one of the doors.

A woman screams from inside. I turn around and hide my face in Vinny's chest, horrified.

"I'm okay." I pull away and walk over to the opening. "Hey honey, I am Etta. We are here to get you out of here."

She stops screaming. "Etta?" she asks.

"We are going to have to pull you out by your legs if that's okay?" I ask her.

She sniffs. "Okay." We pull her out and I don't want to think about the massive splinters she's getting right now.

We put her on her feet and she tilts to the side. She blinks as she adjusts to the light.

I can see cuts all over her body and she's bleeding in random places. "There's no one else in here. I got in trouble earlier." She looks at me, studying me. "You're really Etta?" she asks.

I take the blanket from the prospect and wrap it around her. "Here you go, yes, I am Etta."

Her bottom lip trembles. "For a long time, I've dreamed of you coming to rescue us."

I tear up at that. I lean over and hug her tightly. "You're safe now. You will never have to go back."

She sniffs and I let her cry. Konrad is hovering, unsure of what to do. "You'll take her to one of the medical vans. Once we get everyone cleared out, I will be down," Konrad tells the prospect.

She lets me go and lets the prospect lead her out of the house.

Lane is walking out, carrying a girl bridal-style. "Her legs are broken."

Fuck.

"Let's go into the basement." Konrad takes my hand and we find the secret door. Vinny takes my other hand and we all walk down a huge flight of stairs together.

Once we reach the bottom of the steps, I find the light switch and what I see will forever haunt me.

Hanging from the walls is every single torture device made, blood caking the floor from God knows what.

There are five wooden tables in the middle of the room. Five women are lying on them, tied spread eagle, blood coming from everywhere.

The worst part are the names engraved on their skin— Jezebel, Lilith. Crosses burnt into their skin. There are crosses everywhere. The women are looking at us.

"Who are you?" one of them asks, her beautiful blue eyes showing her fear.

Konrad and Vinny are looking at the ground so the girls aren't scared. "I am Etta. We are here to get you out of here."

One of the girls in the back hisses like she's shocked. "Do you know Henry?" she rushes, trying to get loose.

I walk over to her and I almost fall to the floor. I know right off the bat that this is Robert's mom.

KONRAD

She is alive, but she is in horrible shape and I can see the worst of her problems is she is completely starved.

This is the worst case of malnutrition I have ever seen. "Are you Robert's mom?" I ask.

She nods, crying. "Yes, that's my baby. Is he okay?"

I unhook her and the guys free the other girls. "Yes he is. He's at my home right now. He's the reason we are here. We've been trying to find you."

She sobs and wails and clutches her fists to her chest, overcome with so much pain and emotion. "He is safe, he misses his mom and he's going to be so excited to see you." I try to make her feel better.

"Can I carry you, ma'am?" Vinny asks, holding out a blanket for her. She nods and he wraps her up like a little mummy, lifting her off of the table.

Konrad picks up another girl, and Aiden, Butcher, and Liam come in and get the rest. I walk in front of the guys, so ready to be out of there.

The vans are pulled up close, and the guys lay the girls onto blankets on the ground and cover them with more so they don't feel exposed.

The girls are tagged by who is worst, and Konrad grabs a bag and gets to work, getting all of the girls set up with IVs.

I am overwhelmed.

There are around fifty girls, if not more.

A bunch of vehicles pull up and I start to sigh with relief, thinking it's the girls, but then I realize they couldn't have gotten here this fast.

"Get ready!" I yell and pick up my gun, looking through the scope.

It's the bishops. Now this is what I'm talking about.

The girls start screaming, realizing who just pulled up. I move to stand in front of them and the guys join me. "Get out of the SUV, now!" I yell. Konrad moves next to me, angling his body slightly in front of mine.

I take a deep breath, letting my nerves settle, because if we can capture them, this would be *huge*.

They start to back up when one of the prospects in one of our SUVs pulls up behind them, blocking them in.

"Lane, Kyle," I call. They look at me. "They are some of the leaders—the bishops. The one in the driver's seat is the one that belonged to our church."

They realize what my words mean. This means if we can capture them, we can get information and save so many more women.

One by one we step together, closer and closer.

I can see the fear on their faces as they look at the women on the ground and in our cars. They're realizing how fucked they are.

They were meant to fix these women, now they're realizing we're taking them all and the hell that is going to rain.

Their thinking is wrong. Their hell is not that; it's going to be us. They are going to pay on this earth and in the afterlife.

One thing about them I like is, they don't carry guns. They feel like they're invisible, that nothing can hurt them and that they are fully protected.

Right now, their whole entire world is falling apart. They have spent their days hurting these women.

We all charge to the SUV. Konrad takes my hand and pulls me behind him as he wrenches open one of the doors.

He grabs one of the bishops and throws him onto the ground. I put my foot on his throat, pressing down hard and choking him. "Move, please, I beg you," I taunt him.

His eyes narrow on me, his hand going to my foot and trying to pry it off. His fingers dig into my toes, trying to hurt me.

"Fuck, there's more women."

The bishop below my foot really starts to fight. I stumble when his leg kicks out and he rolls slightly.

I look down at him, glaring. Konrad is standing in front of me going through the papers. "Hey, stop," I tell the guy under my foot when he punches my leg hard.

I cry out, kicking him back, pointing my gun at his head. "Stop it now!" I yell and Konrad whips around at the commotion.

The bishop's face is red from the exertion trying to fight me.

"JEZEBEL!" he roars, pushing me off of him and onto the ground.

I hit the ground, my back slamming into the dirt hard.

Konrad turns around and grips the guy by the hair before he can reach me. He puts his face in front of the bishop's. "Oh, how I am going to love hurting you. You dared to harm her and you will pray for hell," Konrad spits out.

Vinny lifts me off the ground. I know one thing these men are scared of and that's women.

They are so fucking intimidated.

I laugh. "Look how scared he is. What a pathetic excuse for a man," I belittle him.

His face reddens with anger. "You think I'm scared of you? I could take you with my hands tied behind me back."

He tries to run at me. "Let him go. I would love to kick his ass." I smirk at him.

I feel someone walking up behind me. I look back and see my girls. Shaylin walks in front with River.

"Ohh, maybe we should let them all go. Let's show them what women are capable of," River mocks him, winking at one of the bishops lying on the ground.

"Yeah, show them who's boss!" one of the girls yells.

She walks toward me. "Strip him naked," she demands.

I can see the fire in her eyes. Konrad does as she asks, leaving him completely naked.

I look down at his penis. I point at it and all of the girls laugh loudly, completely humiliating him.

His lip trembles, horrified. All of the girls around me have been abused and are taking back their power as they call him every single name in the book. "Shit, I've seen Vienna sausage bigger than him," Robert's mom says last.

I bust out laughing again. River and Shaylin are almost lying on the ground. Gage is laughing harder than everyone; he's practically crazy.

"You think this is bad? What do you think we've felt? I have been here for months," she hisses, stepping up and punching the bishop dead in the face.

I watch in sick fascination as his head snaps back. "Fuck, that felt good, you stupid bitch."

I snort. "I think we just need to tie them up and let the girls have their fun," I joke.

The guys all look at each other. "I don't see why the fuck not. We need to keep one alive for information reasons." Lane shrugs.

"I agree, we will keep this one." Lane picks the bishop off the ground by his feet, throwing him to a prospect.

The guys drag the rest to the middle of the parking lot in front of the house.

One by one, the girls pick themselves up off of the ground, some helping others. "Take their clothes off," one of the girls yells.

I watch as their faces change before my eyes. They are finding their strength and they are taking back what was taken from them.

The prospects do the dirty work. Konrad tucks me into his side. "Are you hurt where he pushed you down?"

I shake my head no. "No, I'm fine, but the best revenge is happening right now in front of our eyes. They are facing their

KONRAD

abusers head on. They're taking back a small part of what was taken from them," I whisper to him.

"What?" Danny asks me.

I smile sadly. "Power."

One of the girls screams and they charge the bishops, surrounding them. I can hear their screams. I can make out the sounds of fists hitting flesh, bones breaking.

"MY BALLS!"

We bust out laughing at that. This continues for close to thirty minutes. We can't even see what's going on, there are so many of them surrounding the bishops.

One by one, the women fall back and collapse onto the ground, exhausted.

We are left with the visuals of men that aren't even men anymore; they are just pieces of meat at this point.

Their heads are lying at weird angles, letting me know one thing. They are dead, never to hurt anyone else.

I walk to the girls and stand in front of them. "You guys ready to go home?" I ask.

"Please," they say.

We all help them to their feet and into the vans. The girls drove them here but the guys will take over driving. We're leaving a girl in each van to make sure that the rescued women feel safe.

It takes close to an hour to get everyone inside of the van. We give them Gatorades and snacks to tide them over until we get back.

We have the chefs currently making meals for them even though it's getting dark outside.

I know it's chaos back at the house getting everything ready, but luckily, I have tons of help because a lot of girls who've been there for a while have taken over duties for us.

Lynn will be there bright and early in the morning with other therapists ready to tackle these girls' mental health issues.

We have seen abuse, but this is just the worst.

I shut the last door of the van and climb inside, and Konrad takes the driver's seat.

He won't leave my side. He has stuck by me all day long and made sure I am okay, protected. I squeeze his hand. "Thank you for protecting me today," I whisper into his ear before kissing his cheek and finding my seat.

He gives me a heated look. I sit in the front, closest to the door. I can feel the eyes of the girls behind me.

I leave on the lights for them so they can see each other. "Are you guys feeling okay? Need anything?"

"I'd kill for a bath," one of the girls says.

A few of the girls laugh. "I just want to lie down and sleep."

I close my eyes, thinking how horrible it would be trying to sleep in one of those fucked up cages.

"Will we have our own beds?" one of them asks.

I nod. "You will have your own beds. You can choose if you want to have one person in your bedroom with you, or we have bunk-bed rooms, but all of them have their own kitchen and bathroom, fully stocked."

They look at me like I'm crazy. "Fully stocked?"

I nod. "Yeah, some of the girls that were rescued years ago are in school to be doctors, nurses, teachers. Some are wanting to join me and do what I do. Some are just mothers, living in peace on the property."

"Wow."

They look at each other in disbelief. "I've wanted this for so long. Etta, we've heard about you for years. How you got out, how you got so many girls out."

"I wish I knew about you guys sooner. When I was eighteen I made a promise that I would end the cults if it's the last thing I do," I tell them.

Looking at their faces, knowing that no one can hurt them again, that makes it worth it.

"I have a daughter. She's four years old. Can we rescue her?" the one closest to me asks, her eyes bright with tears.

"Tomorrow we will get all of your information and we will get your loved ones one by one."

They start crying, and I feel utterly useless right now, but I hope those tears dry up once I reunite those who are separated.

The girls all fall asleep and I move to the front with Konrad, cutting off the lights so they can rest.

He reaches over, taking my hand, bringing the back of it to his mouth and kissing me. "Darlin', you are so fucking strong. I've been in awe of you today." He looks at me with such sincerity.

I lean over and rest my forehead on his shoulder, letting myself be vulnerable for a second. "You make me happy," I admit.

I see his beautiful happy smile from the corner of my eye. "Darlin', you make me so much more than happy."

I shake my head, smiling ear to ear, my heart happy, butterflies in my stomach. "Once we're home, I'm going to run you a hot bath, I'll find us some food and turn on a movie. You deserve to relax, baby."

Dear God, I almost fall to the ground in a puddle. "You are amazing," I whisper, not wanting the girls to hear.

"Baby, that's all you. Look at what you did today. Look how far you have come in life. You made this from the bottom, turned it to this so you can help all of these people."

God, my heart burns as his words hit close to home. "You're going to make me cry."

"Don't cry. One thing I can't handle is your tears, honey. "

In this very moment, I truly realize I am a complete and utter goner for this man. His face actually shows his pain as he glances over at me.

He truly cares for me.

The rest of the ride back home is so long, the girls are so

uncomfortable, they're wincing with every move and bump on the road.

The line of vans pulls to a stop in front of the gate, waiting for the person in front to put in the code and check in with the prospect there.

I stand up and walk to the back with the girls, turning on the light so they can adjust.

"How's everyone feeling?" I ask, but they're too busy looking out of the window at the houses along the driveway to the main houses.

"Who lives in these houses?" one of the girls asks.

"Most are newer and no one lives in these yet. A lot of the girls have readjusted to new housing. Some live alone with their kids."

They look at me in shock. "What? They have their own homes?"

I smile. "Yes, you will too, but first you will be staying in the main house until you're adjusted."

I can tell they're trying to wrap their head around the idea of that life. I know once I left the cult it was so hard to learn new things.

The van stops and I step out. Konrad helps the girls out of the vans, making sure they don't fall.

"Alright everyone, follow me." I motion for all of the girls to follow me—the ones that can walk, that is. Some are in the medical vans and they will have to be carried in last.

"I'm going to stay with medical to check on the girls," Konrad tells me.

Inside of the house, I'm relived at the amount of help on hand. "Girls, thank you so much for this. These rescued girls are in bad shape," I warn them.

The house is filled with the smell of soup, and my stomach growls from not eating in hours.

I split the rescued girls off in groups and they follow one of my girls to their rooms to clean up. We've called in some nurses to make sure every girl is looked after and to assess if they need more medical treatment.

There was no way to make sure everyone got checked over there. We needed to get them out before something happened and anyone else showed up.

We got lucky it was just the bishops—those fuckers were useless.

Once the girls are all upstairs, I look at the empty main room. Shaylin walks up to me, hugging me into her side. "How are you holding up?" she asks.

I rub my eyes, sighing loudly. "It never gets easier." She nods, accepting that response. "I'm going to head up and make sure everyone is adjusting okay. Want to head up with me?" I ask.

"Fuck yeah."

I laugh. Shaylin has been a friend of mine for a while. She took me under her wing and she helped me learn how to defend myself. She was the one who taught me how to shoot.

We walk upstairs, and once we reach the top of the landing, we are hit with an ear-piercing scream.

I gasp in shock at the sound and I run toward the sound. I can hear the thundering footsteps behind us as the guys run up the stairs.

I push open the door and I see one of the younger girls in the corner of the room, holding onto a pillow. I run to her. "Honey, you're okay!" I whisper to her, trying to break through the panic she is feeling.

Her eyes aren't on me but on the TV hanging on the wall. "Hey," I try again and she finally, slowly, looks over to me, and the look on her face takes my breath away.

"What's the matter, honey? Did something happen?" I ask, sitting on the ground beside her.

Her hair is plastered to the side of her face from the sweat, tears, and God only knows what else.

I help fasten the blanket around her shoulders to make sure she feels secure. She points to the man's face on the screen.

I look over and see the chief of police talking about some kind of crime that happened in town.

"What's the matter, honey?"

Her eyes are filled with tears. "That is my daddy."

Wait what? Then why was she there? I look over at the guys in horror because I actually know the man and he has been trying to find his daughter since she was twelve years old when she went missing.

"Sweetheart, you need to tell me," I tell her in a gentle, soothing tone.

She sniffs. "I was taken from outside of the school. My mom was late picking me up and I was carried into a van years ago."

I close my eyes. "Sweetheart, I am so sorry." I pull her over and hold her as she weeps from all of the pain she has suffered.

Konrad is hovering by the door, waiting to make sure she is okay. "Okay, honey, I need to ask you something."

She nods. "How old are you now?"

She wipes her eyes with the back of her hand. "I'm fourteen. I know I look older. I was taken two years ago." Her eyes get glassy as she sinks into her mind.

Fuck, I hate this so much.

"One more thing." She looks at me once more. "Do you want me to call your dad?"

She is shocked by my words. "You know my dad?" she asks, sitting up straighter.

I push her hair over her shoulder. "I do know him, honey. He has been working with us since you were taken."

She nods. "I want my daddy please," she begs, tears finally falling from her eyes. "I just want to go home. I tried to not think of home but I just want my daddy."

My throat thickens. "Okay, honey. I'll call him right now. I am going to turn the water on for you. There's clothes on the counter. I'll check on you in a bit."

I help her off of the floor and she walks into the bathroom, the door locking behind her.

I run out of the room. I need to tell Kyle, since this is the police chief. Kyle is standing in the main room.

"Kyle!" I yell and run down the stairs, stopping in front of him.

He grips my shoulders. "What is it?" he asks.

I am shaking from all of the emotions I am feeling. "I just found Olivia—she was who is screaming. She saw her dad on TV."

His face shows his shock. We have searched and searched for her, but never in a million years did I think she was in the cult, that they had taken her.

This is going to make me reanalyze everything I know about them—this is different.

"She wants me to call him."

"Fuck, how bad is she?" Kyle asks.

It makes me mad that I didn't see her. There were so many girls in that short period of time, she just slipped through the cracks.

I close my eyes, hating this. "She doesn't look that good. Once she's out of the shower I will have someone check her."

Kyle has known her since she was little. He and the police chief are best friends and her going missing affected everyone in this town because stuff like that just doesn't happen in Raleigh.

"Can I go wait outside of her door?"

"Let me call her dad and I'll take you to her. I'm sure she recognizes you."

He nods. "I gotta tell Chrystal." He takes out his phone and calls his wife.

This is heartbreaking.

Your daughter being missing is the worst thing imaginable, but knowing what she has suffered all of this time?

That makes it hurt even worse.

Because it is the worst nightmare come true.

I step outside, breathing in the cool night air. The door opens and Konrad steps out. He pulls me over to a chair and into his lap.

"I know this is hard, baby." He rubs my back. I let my head sink for a minute, letting myself gather my emotions, feeling the pain before I shut it off.

I lean back, kissing his cheek softly and showing my thanks. I dial Brian's number, and a few rings later he picks up. "Hey Etta, how did the bust go?"

I clench my eyes closed, hating this.

"Are you sitting down?" My voice comes through with no emotions.

"What is it?" he demands. I can hear a door opening and closing. I know he's moving into his office.

"We've found her. She's here at the compound. Olivia is alive."

I can hear crashing. "Oh my God," he says into the phone. I can hear some guys yelling and I know he's at work.

"Is she bad?" he asks. I can hear the fear in his voice.

"We don't know the full extent yet, but she wants you."

"I'll be there in thirty minutes." He hangs up and I stuff the phone into my pocket. "I need to go check on her."

Konrad takes my hand and walks me up the stairs, Kyle right behind us. "Let me walk in first to make sure she is okay."

They hang back as I open the door, stepping inside as Olivia is walking out of the bathroom.

I have to suck in a breath because now I can tell for sure she's Olivia. I couldn't even recognize her under the filth.

"Your dad is on his way," I tell her, and she sits on the edge of the bed, taking the blanket and wrapping it around her.

"Someone here wants to see you, if that's okay?" I ask her. "He's a male."

She looks scared for a second. "Stay with me please?" she begs.

"I won't leave you, honey." I run my hand down her wet hair. "Come in!" I yell.

The door opens and I watch her reaction to seeing Kyle. She bursts out crying and runs to him. "Uncle Kyle."

He lifts her off the ground, holding her tightly as she cries and cries. "I have missed you, pumpkin," he tells her, kissing the top of her head.

His eyes are looking straight ahead, fire inside of them. I know that there will be hell to pay for this and I know one thing — I want a part of that.

There is a knock on the door and it opens. "The female doctor is here."

This part sucks. I was terrified out of my mind when Lani and Vinny took me to the doctor, but hopefully it will be easier for Olivia because she grew up in the normal world first.

Olivia sniffs and steps back from Kyle. "Let's get it over with," she says without emotion. I know she's turning it off.

Kyle steps out, looking at me pleadingly. I know he wants me to stay with her.

I nod once, letting him know that I will stay with her. I hold her hand, talking her through everything as she gets checked, tested and then gets her blood work done. It only takes a few minutes, but I know in her head it feels like forever.

I hear a loud truck outside and her eyes widen. Her dad is here. I move to the foot of the bed, my heart pounding, waiting for the guys to bring him up.

The door is pushed open. Brian's eyes go straight to his daughter. "My baby." He walks to her and starts to pick her up but stops. "Can I touch you, baby?"

She jumps up and he lifts her. "I missed you so much, Daddy," she cries, holding onto him for dear life.

I have to look away, the scene too raw. I look at Kyle, who is barely holding it together, and Konrad looks just as devastated.

"Can she go home?" Brian asks me.

"Yes, but I recommend her coming back here every day for therapy. She has been seen by a doctor and we will have those results soon," I inform him.

He closes his eyes, hugging her a little tighter. "Want to go home?" he asks.

"I really want that."

He takes her hand and Olivia slowly walks from the room. I know she's in pain. Brian bends over and carries her down the stairs.

"Come on, honey, you've done all you can do." Konrad takes my hand and lets me into my apartment on the top floor.

I let him drag me; I am so emotionally drained.

He sets me on the bed and walks into the bathroom. I stare at the doorway he just walked in.

I notice a duffle bag on the chair. I walk over and open it. It's full of clothes for Konrad.

I guess he's planning on staying for a while, and I have to admit, I'm not mad at it.

"I've started the bath for you. I'm going to run downstairs for a shower. I want you to relax—no more worrying about the others, okay?"

"Okay." I let out a deep breath. "Thank you." I am totally exhausted and most of it is just mental exhaustion.

I sit in the warm bubbles, closing my eyes and wanting to forget this day even happened.

Konrad

KONRAD

A PIERCING SCREAM wakes me up from my dead sleep. I look over at Etta, who is fighting in her sleep, her face looks like she's in pain and she's gasping for air, like she's having a panic attack.

"Etta, baby." I try to wake her up and it doesn't even faze her. Fuck.

I put my hands on her face. "Baby, wake up. You're having a nightmare," I try a little louder and her eyes open. The complete and utter terror on her face makes me lose my fucking breath.

"Are you okay?" I ask, pushing her hair off of her face.

I can feel her shaking under me. Whatever she was dreaming was bad. She shakes her head no, my heart breaking a little.

Fuck, she is wrecking me.

She wraps her arms around my neck, pulling me down until I'm practically lying on top of her. "I'm too heavy," I tell her, trying to take my weight off of her.

"No, you're just right. You make me feel safe."

Fuck, if that didn't make me feel a hundred feet tall. She breathes deep, in and out, trying to calm herself down.

I lean up, staring down at her. "Baby, what did you dream?" I don't want to fucking know, but I know that speaking about it may help her.

A tear falls from her eyes. I catch it with my lips, pressing a kiss there and resting my forehead against hers, giving her all the time she needs.

"I have PTSD. Today just made it worse. Today was hard." The pain on her face is real. "I dreamed that I was fourteen again, when I was forced to marry. I have that dream usually every night I have a mission, but this one was extra bad because that could have been me..." She trails off. I can't fucking fathom that she could have gone through that.

Fuck, I hate this shit. "Fuck, I wish I could take it from you, the hurt you have suffered. I would do anything." I whisper the last part, my heart fucking hurting so fucking bad for her, for all of the girls here.

I spent many years of my life on missions, protecting and serving this country from those who dared to harm it, but this shit? Right in the fucking US? I will stop this shit.

I wish I could have protected her from it. Life isn't fucking fair. "You being here with me, taking care of me, it's taking a small bit of the hurt from my heart a little at a time."

That shit hits me right in the heart. "Baby." I shake my head, leaning down, kissing her, wanting her to feel everything I'm feeling right now.

I am so fucked when it comes to her.

She has wrecked me.

The Next Day
Etta

MY PHONE RINGS and I pick it up when I see it's the doctor from yesterday. She usually sends the labs over. If I get a phone call, then it means she has some news.

We always send in swabs in case there is DNA. Usually there is none, but sometimes in rare cases we get pings in the system. It's rare, though, as most of the guys in the cults are off the grid.

"Hey, what's up?" I ask.

I've been busy all day long making sure the girls have everything they need.

"We have a ping in the system for Olivia and a few of the other girls," she says, and she has a weird tone.

"Who is it?" I ask, putting a book one of the girls was reading on the shelf.

"It's Randy Henderson."

Fuck, this is *bad*.

Konrad overhears because the call is on speaker phone, and before I can utter a word, he is running out of the house.

Randy is the high school principal at the school that Olivia went to. Another of the girls we rescued goes there too and I have gotten calls from other girls that go to that school.

Wait...

My eyes widen as I connect the dots. I run out of the house, catching Konrad before he leaves, hopping on the back of his bike.

This is not fucking good. At all.

7

KONRAD

That fucking name.

It's running through my fucking head because this stupid fucker had played all of us.

He cried on fucking camera, begging for Olivia to be returned home and he was fucking raping her all of this time.

The betrayal that little girl must have felt, the hurt she experienced on an emotional level.

I make it to the Devil Souls club house in half of the time on my bike. I help Etta off of the bike and into the club house.

Lane jumps off of the couch with Amelia when he spots me. "We need to get Kyle. We have information."

Lane looks at Etta; she's pale from the information she has gotten. Lane runs off and Amelia looks unsure of what to do.

I pull Etta into me, hugging her to my chest. She settles against me, arms right around me.

Kyle runs into the room with his brothers and he motions for me to come into the conference room. I hold Etta's hand and lead her into the room.

Everyone sits down. Etta doesn't though.

Her jaw is set. I can see the fire in her eyes, the need to

avenge Olivia. I know the fucking work she put into finding that little girl.

"They found DNA on Olivia and a few of the other girls." She shakes her head like she can't fucking believe this.

Kyle sits up straighter. "Who is it?"

Etta walks toward him. "Randy fucking Henderson."

The silence around the room is deafening as everyone wraps their head around what the fuck is happening.

Kyle stands up, lifting the chair and throwing it against the wall.

Etta flinches hard at the sudden anger from Kyle. I pull her into me, pissed off that he scared her, Devil Souls MC president be damned. "Chill the fuck out, you scared her," I growl at him.

I see Lane shift beside me and I know even though they are good fucking friends, he is my brother. I helped raise him.

Kyle looks at Etta with regret. "I'm sorry, sweetheart. She's just a few years older than my daughter, they grew up together," he tells her gently.

She reaches out and touches his arm. "I understand, Kyle. This hurts all of us. I worked with him alone, repeatedly. I have spoken to him about the cult, the horrors of it." She clears her throat.

Fuck, the pain on her face is raw.

"He cried for her and the other girls that went missing in Raleigh. He played me, he manipulated me. I am fucking sick to my stomach." She touches her stomach.

She looks around the room at each and every man. "We have made a lot of fuckers suffer for the things they have done, but this person, he is going to feel the wrath of a father and a whole fucking MC. His end is going to be the worst, because he fucked with all of us."

The guys around the room nod, agreeing with her.

This is different, this is personal.

"Looks like it's time to reap, boys." I grin at that, more than fucking ready to cause shit and raise hell.

Etta

I HAVE BEEN TRAINED in a lot of ways, but Liam personally trained me. I wanted to be knowledgeable in everything.

I am in the basement as they track down Randy. I had a prospect bring in a small cage for Randy to enjoy his long stay.

He's not going to die today nor tomorrow. He's going to know the pain of what Olivia suffered in those damn cages.

The claustrophobia—he's going to be right next to the fucking bishop.

Hell, I may make them hurt each other. What fun that would be.

Right now, I am not Etta. I am someone different, someone who tastes revenge. It's so deep and thick inside of me.

Liam is right next to me, making a plan of action.

But first everyone is going to have their fun. I can't watch that. I can't stomach it, but I take satisfaction in what is going to happen.

He is not human in my eyes and he won't be treated as such.

Poor Olivia—the nights I have lost sleep, her father tracing every little step trying to find his baby.

He did this.

He caused the kind of suffering that nothing can soothe, but I can surely try.

"Konrad is a doctor, so we can use him to keep him alive," Liam says to me. I hear a door opening and the sounds of yelling.

It's time.

Konrad

WE FIND him on his couch, lying there in his underwear without a worry in the world.

We bust in the door and he sits up, relaxing when he sees us. "Hey guys, did something happen?"

He speaks to us like we're his friends, when really he is shit beneath our toes. "Oh, something happened alright. We found Olivia." Kyle walks up from behind me, with Brian right on his fucking heels.

His face changes to one of utter horror as he connects the fucking dots. "Looks like your time is up, Randy boy," I taunt him and grab him by his hair. I cut off his underwear, knowing that it will humiliate him.

"Better get used to not having one of those." I shove his face toward his dick. I laugh at him gagging.

Brian's eyes are on him. I can feel that shit, that anger is so deep. I drag him out, and he sobs and screams the whole time.

I grip him by the face, pushing him against the van. "Your fucking sobs make me happy. Keep it up." I squeeze his face hard, and his eyes roll back from the pain.

I throw him to the prospects. "Keep the air on arctic in the fucking back." They nod and toss him.

Brian is eyeing the van. I know it's taking everything in him not to tear after him. Olivia is at the compound for therapy today.

"In time," I tell him, and he gives me a hard look before nodding.

"How do you feel about me being a brother?" Brian asks Kyle.

Kyle looks at him in surprise. "I've been meaning to ask for a long-ass time. Now is the time, because the things I am going to do to him… The chief of police is no more, not after this."

Kyle looks at his brothers surrounding him, and they all nod. "Fuck yeah, brother, no need to prospect. The patch is yours."

Brian walks over to his bike, climbing on. Pulling up behind that van, I know he is going to protect that van with his life until he can take a life.

Etta

AT THE FIRST glimpse of Randy, I see how terrified he is. He is completely naked and I am disgusted by that.

I walk over to my cages. Some are so small that he may have to break some bones to even get inside. "Randy, look at your new home." I grin, waving my arm like I'm on a fucking game show.

Randy looks at the cages in horror. "Not too keen on them now, are you? But don't worry. You'll get used to it." I grin at him.

"Me and Liam have gone through and selected the best tools for you. Nothing but the best for you." I walk over and grab a cow castration tool with a band on it.

"Now this is my favorite tool." I rub it lovingly.

I hear a weird, wet sound, then I scrunch up my nose at him pissing all over himself and the floor.

Konrad looks at me in amusement, completely unfazed. "Well shit, I think we just need to hand him over to Etta," Liam jokes.

I put the tool back on the table. "I'm going to leave now. Have fun," I call and walk out of the room.

I go into the kitchen and make some dinner for the guys with the girls. We all pretend we have no clue what's going on downstairs.

Shaylin walks in with Tiana, who is ten years old now. "Hi, sweet girl."

She smiles at me, her ponytail swinging. She has grease all over her face and is completely obsessed with working on motorcycles like her dad Butcher.

The first time I saw Butcher I was terrified of him—he is huge, completely covered in tattoos, and so intimidating.

The second I saw him with his sweet daughter and the way he treats Shaylin and their son, it completely changed my mind.

All of these guys did.

Lynn and I were both so jaded when it came to men—all we knew were the horrors we had faced and what others had.

They changed our lives.

They are all my best friends. Did I ever think that would happen? Definitely not. "Do you guys want to come watch a movie while the food cooks?" Alisha asks.

She is the sweetest and so is her mom Adeline, who is Smiley's old lady. She is a huge help in the compound. She loves kids and she's a mother figure to everyone.

We all settle under blankets in front of the TV, Tiana scooting in closer to me, wanting cuddles.

Konrad

Randy's arms are hanging above his head. They dragged the bishop out of his cage and he's hanging the same exact way.

The bishop is already fucked up. He has been here since yesterday and everyone has come down to fuck with him to get more information.

One thing is for sure, we have not been asking all of the right questions. "Are you responsible for the girls going missing at your high school?" I ask Randy.

He clenches his mouth shut, along with his eyes. I laugh. "Please don't speak, you're just going to make it so much more funner." The guys laugh with me.

We all agree. We love that they don't talk. The longer they hold on, the better it is for us. It becomes a competition to see who can get them to talk.

In the end it's usually Liam. The fucker has been trained in torture and he did that shit when he was a SEAL.

Brian stares at Randy. He fucking stares at him in a way that is promising so much fucking pain.

Randy has his eyes closed like that is going to help him. Kyle has fucking helped Brian raise Olivia. They grew up together.

Liam steps forward, smiling, Torch standing next to him. Liam walks to the castration tool that Etta had. "I don't know about you guys, but I think it's time for us to put this on. It does take a while for it to work." Liam puts the band on the clamp, opening it and closing it.

He puts on a pair of gloves and walks to Randy. He screams at the top of his lungs, trying to kick at Liam when he gets closer.

"Answer the question," I say once again.

It isn't going to stop it from happening, but it doesn't hurt to let them think that. Randy looks at the bishop, whose eyes are glassy from the trauma. Fucking pussy.

Butcher is standing next to me, Techy on the other side. Trey and Vinny are hanging beside me also.

Randy kicks one last time before realizing that it's not going to help him. "Wait!" he yells when Liam bends over. "What do you want to know?" he asks, sweat pouring down his face.

"Are you responsible for girls going missing from your school?" I ask my first question again.

Randy pales at my question and swallows hard. His arms are shaking from being over his head for so long. I know he's losing feeling.

He looks around the room at our faces. "I have been the one to set up contact, I choose the girls," he says really low, like it will soften the blow.

Brian's fists clench at his sides but he holds still. "How long have you been doing this?"

He looks at Torch and Liam suddenly, then away. That was fucking weird. Kyle looks at Torch. "How long?" I repeat.

"Over ten years."

Liam jerks like he has been shot and so does Torch. "Who was the first girl?" Torch steps forward, staring him down. "Who was the first girl?" he repeats.

Randy looks like he's almost in tears. "Paisley."

Everyone in the room almost falls to the fucking floor. The janitor that attacked her outside of her school…

Liam doesn't speak, just moves.

He puts the band around his balls and lets go. The scream that Randy lets out is one of pure agony—one that can't be matched.

Liam takes another band, grabbing Randy's tongue and pulling it out of his mouth. He puts another band around his tongue, softening his screams.

They started wars years ago and we didn't fucking know it. Randy screams and screams.

We watch. We revel in it.

It's only the beginning.

They started the war, but we are ending it.

8

ETTA

They make their way out of the basement hours later. "Ready to go home?" Torch asks Kayla. He is pissed the fuck off.

A second later Liam slams the door open, making his way to Paisley, who is sitting next to me. She stands up and walks to him. If it's even possible, Liam is more pissed off than Torch.

She is confused and so am I. All of the guys are looking at her differently. Liam pulls her to the side with Torch, her dad.

Something must have happened down there. I walk to Konrad. "What happened in there?" I grip the front of his cut, worried about what has happened.

Paisley's face changes to one of horror, the anger on Torch's and Liam's faces has me catching my breath.

"Do you remember when Paisley was attacked? At school when she was sixteen?" he asks.

Then it hits me like a ton of bricks. "Oh my God, are you telling me that this has been going on for this long?"

Butcher nods beside me, holding Tiana tightly. I know he's thinking what if that was his daughter.

Lord help the man that dared to hurt that little girl. She has the whole MC at her back.

Konrad tucks me under his chin, all of us silent, watching the moment between all of them.

"I hope he is hurting right now," I tell Konrad softly.

Butcher looks over to me, smiling, which I have never seen him do before. "Hurting doesn't touch what he's feeling."

I look up at Konrad, who has the same sinister smile on his face. "Ready to head back?" Konrad asks me.

I nod. I'm exhausted and I need to check on all of the girls including Robert's mom and introduce the two later.

She wanted to be kept apart from him until she looks presentable. She didn't want to scare him and I understand that. She was one of the worst we have seen, but her only thoughts were of Robert.

I can't fathom as a mother knowing your child was out there and you were taken from him.

Henry is still alive; he is in his very own cage at the moment. I had one shipped to where he is being held; he is still very useful with the information he is giving.

I am not in control of that. That is Liam's job. Once we get someone like that in our custody, he is handed over to Liam.

We have rarely had cases of women in charge, and if that happens, they are handed over to Shaylin, whom I almost think is scarier than Liam at times.

Brian walks over to me. I can see the deep, horrible pain in his eyes but I can see it's lightened a bit. I know the fact that he is getting some sort of revenge for his daughter is helping that.

But I know it will never go away, not fully. I know the worst part is the guilt that he didn't protect his daughter.

Olivia's mother is a piece of shit and I am not saying that lightly. She treated Olivia like shit, so Olivia took a walk to her dad's after they had a fight. Her mom broke her phone so she couldn't call and that's how she was picked up on the side of the road.

Just like that, something can change your whole entire world.

Nothing can change the things that have happened to her—they can't be taken back, but there is hope at the end of it, it just takes a long time to get there.

"I'm going to head back with you guys to get Olivia," Brian tells me and Konrad.

I reach out and put my hand on his arm. "That's fine with us. Are you feeling okay?" I ask.

He looks up at the ceiling before nodding. "I'm fine." The lie is so huge, I can feel it.

Konrad shakes his head at me to not say more, but there is nothing else I can say. Words can't fix this.

Konrad puts his hand on my hips and rubs them.

I try not to show how much that touch is affecting me. Turning around, I wrap my arms around his neck, stand on my tiptoes and kiss him.

I kiss him in front of everyone. He lifts me off of the ground, pulling me tighter against him.

Everyone around us disappears—all it is right now is us.

I put my hands on his cheeks, loving the movement of his mouth against mine. It's heady.

I finally pull back, kissing him one last time on the cheek and I smile happily at him.

"Damn, girl," Shaylin yells, and I blush deeply at that.

Konrad laughs and tucks my face into his chest. "Stop being so fucking cute."

My eyes glow happily at the compliment. As I look around, I see two angry faces and I swallow hard at the sight.

Trey and Vinny are standing side by side, arms crossed across their chests. I suck in my lips and look away.

"You do know that's my fucking sister. Etta, what are you doing?" Trey asks loudly, talking to me in a tone I have never heard from him.

KONRAD

It gets so eerily quiet and everyone stops talking.

Trey has always been extremely overly protective of me and Lynn. Vinny is my brother, but Trey acts like my father and he has from the second I met him.

Did he not know me and Konrad are seeing each other?

I see Vinny wince. Oh fuck, he didn't tell Trey! Trey is used to seeing me with the guys but never like this.

I step away from Konrad, getting pissed off that they're acting this way, but Konrad is completely unfazed by all of it.

He gently sets me to the side and walks up to Trey and Vinny. "Listen, you may not like it, but Etta is mine. She has been from the second I laid eyes on her; I felt that shit all the way to my core. I have never claimed a woman before her. You can try to intimidate me." Konrad stops talking, his jaw set. I know he's pissed off. "But you don't make her feel ashamed. Do what you want to me but not her, not Etta." He says my name with such affection.

Vinny's whole face softens at Konrad's words. Trey swallows hard and he looks at me like I've broken his heart before his face softens. "I didn't mean to take a tone with you, sweetheart. My heart hurts because you've grown up."

He laughs, but his eyes are misty like he's trying to hold back tears. I walk to him and hug him tightly. "You're like my dad. I understand why you reacted that way." I don't want him to beat himself up.

He stiffens in my arms at my words before he practically melts into me. "You and Lynn are like my daughters. I will forever see you as such and it hurts my heart a little seeing you locked up with Konrad." He kisses the top of my head and I hug him a little tighter.

I can't help but laugh a little at his choice of words. Trey's arms feel like home, but so do Konrad's.

Vinny laughs with me and tugs the both of us into a tight

hug. They let me go and Konrad immediately steps in, taking me into his arms. "Bye, guys!"

Trey watches me leave with Konrad. I wave one last time before the door shuts. "I'm making you dinner tonight." Konrad puts the helmet on my head and I smile, holding onto him.

Brian follows us back to the compound, in a truck this time. Inside the compound in one of the living rooms I find Olivia with Robert's mom Maci.

Olivia perks up once she sees us and her dad. "Hi Daddy, I want to introduce you to Maci. She took care of me there, protected me." Her voice softens when she gets to the last part.

I can understand now why she was in such horrible shape. She got it from caring for others.

Brian swallows hard when he looks at Maci. He lifts his hand, running it through his hair, but his hand is shaking. Hard.

He visibly swallows. "It's nice to meet you," he tells her.

She smiles and I'm taken aback by how unbelievably beautiful she is. "It's nice to meet you. Olivia has talked about you so much," she says sweetly.

Brian's eyes are hard as he looks at her. It's like he's in disbelief that she's even speaking to him.

He finally collects himself, smiling. "It's nice to meet you too, angel."

Lord have mercy.

I watch this happen before my eyes. Olivia is just as shocked, but I can see her happiness that they are getting along.

I know that Maci is a huge part of her life and she wants everyone to get along in it.

"Maci, are you ready?" I ask her.

Her face shows her nervousness with what is about to happen, but she nods. I got the backstory this morning of why she was there.

Henry was trying to hurt Robert. She caught him trying to hit him and she knocked him out with a frying pan.

She tried to run but she was taken and Robert was forced to stay. Her story is heartbreaking.

I help her off the couch and I am reminded of how beautiful she is. She's wearing a stunning white dress, and her hair is long, blonde, and hanging down her back, a perfect complement to her piercing green eyes.

"It was nice to meet you, Brian. See you tomorrow, Olivia." She leans forward, hugging her. "Make sure you eat a snack before bed and your medicine, okay?"

Olivia nods. "I will, good luck," she tells her and Maci nods, smiling.

I slowly walk her to one of the guest houses next door. This is where she's going to be living if she wants it.

"He's in here?" she asks, confused, looking at the small two-bedroom house.

"Well, this is your house if you want it." Her face shows her shock. She grips the wall like she's holding herself up.

She looks from me to Konrad. "I don't know how I will ever thank you guys." She shakes her head from side to side in disbelief.

I take her hand, squeezing slightly. "You can be happy."

Maci is just twenty-one years old. She had Robert when she was fifteen years old and married at fourteen.

I push open the door and one of the house moms pats me on the shoulder before walking out the door.

I see Robert sitting on the couch in front of the TV. "Robert, I have someone here to see you," I interrupt his show.

He looks up at me before his eyes go to his mother. "Mommy," he whispers so softly, before he jumps off of the couch and over to her, his face going into her belly.

Maci is sobbing hard. Konrad kisses my temple as I hold back tears of my own. "God, I missed you so much, baby." Maci holds him a little tighter.

"I missed you too, Mommy," he whispers, his little body shaking.

Maci pulls back, bending at her knees, touching his face. "I want to look at you. You've gotten so big."

He smiles. He has the same eyes as her. "I'm sorry Daddy sent you away because I was bad."

Fuck, that takes a little piece of my heart.

She shakes her head no. "No, baby, it is not your fault. What matters is we are together forever and nothing can change that," she whispers to him.

He nods. "I helped them find you." He's pretty proud of the fact.

Maci smiles, holding his hand. "I heard about that, baby. I am so proud of you," she praises him.

I know that she is the best mom to this little boy. It makes me so happy that they are together again.

"I'll let you guys be alone. The kitchen is fully stocked. Come to the main house if you need anything." We leave them alone together and let them get readjusted.

"I'm going to go on up and cook dinner." Konrad kisses me on the cheek, and I watch him leave.

An hour later I make my way up to my apartment. The second I open the door I'm hit with the amazing smell of food.

Konrad peeks his head around the corner to double-check and see if it's me. "Dinner is almost ready if you want to shower really quick. I have some clothes on the sink for you."

I don't think I will ever get used to the fact that he does things for me like this. "Thank you."

I notice that his hair is wet from showering already. I lean over and kiss his bare shoulder before stepping into the bathroom.

KONRAD

I don't bother with locking the door. I trust him.

After my shower, I take the clothes he laid out for me and I laugh at the sight of his clothes in my hand.

Not going to deny the fact I love being in his clothes. I love the way he smells. I pull the shirt on and a pair of panties of mine that he grabbed from my drawer.

Opening the bathroom door, I step out to a beautiful sight. He has set the table with candles and is placing our plates on the table.

"Konrad, you did all of this?" I ask, walking over to him happily.

He smiles. "Darlin', it's not a thing."

But then he whips out a bouquet of flowers—how did he even get these? "Konrad, this is too much."

"Sweetheart, you deserve flowers every single day." He bends over, kissing me gently on the cheek.

I close my eyes, leaning into the kiss. "Thank you so much," I say, my hand on his arm.

I take the flowers into the kitchen, grab a vase from the top shelf, and put them in water. I touch the petals lovingly.

The way he spoke to Trey earlier, how he claimed me right in front of everyone, meant a lot.

I didn't have any doubt where I stood in his life, but hearing the words and the way he admitted it to everyone meant a lot to me.

He pulls out my chair for me, helping me sit and pushing my chair in for me. He opens a bottle of wine and pours me a glass.

"You're so sweet. Thank you so much." I take a drink of the wine.

He takes a long pull of his beer. "Darlin, get used to it." He reaches over the table and takes my hand for a second before he starts eating the pasta he made.

I take a bite myself. I close my eyes, savoring the amazing

food. "God, this is probably one of the best things I have ever eaten."

His dimple pops out with his smile. "Darlin', you're too sweet. Would you like to go meet my parents this week?" he asks me, throwing me for a loop.

I twirl the pasta around my fork. "I would really like that. I'd like to see where you live too."

"Do you like horses?" he asks.

I nod. "I've always wanted to learn to ride but haven't had the opportunity. I've thought about getting horses for the girls here for therapy reasons."

"That's a really great idea—rescue some horses from slaughterhouses and things like that. Both could benefit."

I point my fork at him. "That literally is an amazing idea!" I immediately start getting excited about the idea.

The rest of dinner is made up of small talk about his parents and what they're like. I'm excited to meet the people who made such a special person.

We fall into bed, not even bothering with the dishes. All I want is to be curled up in bed with him right now.

He turns on a random movie and leans around me, arm pressed into the mattress by my head.

His eyes search my face. It's like he's searching for any sign of discomfort. His free hand touches the side of my face soothingly. "Darlin', I have never seen someone as beautiful as you. You are beautiful through and through." He puts his hands over my heart. "Your heart though? You're an angel."

"Konrad, you say such kind things to me." I lean forward, kissing him first this time.

He takes over immediately. His fingers drift oh so softly across my throat, my cheekbone to the back of my head, fingers digging deep into my hair.

With every single pull of his lips, every movement, fire burns between my legs.

I want him in a way I have never wanted someone before.

I shift under him until he's settled right between my legs. I can feel his hardness pressed against my panties through his sweatpants.

A chill runs through my body at his touch, and the kiss turns sweltering.

I lean back, gasping for air, trying not to tilt my hips and feel him pressed against me harder.

I grip the blankets beside me, trying to gain control before I embarrass myself.

His hand moves to my hip, touching the bare skin there, to my thigh. He hefts my legs until I'm opened more for him.

His lips move to my neck and my eyes widen at the new sensation. It drives me crazy. I grip the back of his head, the small, pulling kisses moving across my skin, stealing my breath.

I tilt my hips, not to able to stand it anymore, and he presses against my clit. Oh God.

He stops all movements and moves above me, eyes staring deep into mine. His face is completely serious.

"Etta, how far are you wanting to take this? Do you want me to stop?"

God, the respect I have for this man. I am so used to people just taking.

I lift my hand, cupping his face, my heart so full. "Make love to me, Konrad. I'm ready. You make me feel so safe, cared for." I pour my heart out, showing him exactly how I feel.

I push some of his hair off of his forehead. "I've not been with anyone since before; you're the first. In a way, this is my first time ever." I want him to know how much of a big deal this is.

His head falls. I know he's affected by my words. "Angel, you're giving me the biggest fucking gift ever. You are the best thing on this earth and you're all mine."

That brings the waterworks. A tear falls from my eye and down my cheek. He catches it before it can hit my pillow.

He kisses me once more. This time it's filled with so much emotion, so much everything.

Words sometimes aren't enough, but the touch of someone is literally everything.

He sits up on his knees, looking down at me. "Anytime you want me to stop, slow down, let me know and I will stop instantly," he reassures me.

I sit up and lift my shirt over my head, leaving me just in my underwear and bra. He looks me up and down.

I have scars all over my body, but under his eyes I feel beautiful. "God, you're beautiful." His hands drift down my sides all the way to my knees.

"I'm going to take off the rest of your clothes," he tells me.

I lift my hips, and he pulls down my underwear and takes off my bra. I am completely naked, but I'm not scared.

I know without a doubt that he's going to take care of me. His eyes are heated, I can tell that he wants me.

God, how I want him to take me.

He licks his lips. "God, I could eat you up." He slides down the bed, spreading my legs. "I'll do just that." He gives me a wicked grin and dips his head.

I clench my eyes closed, feeling nervous for the first time. I have never done this before and I'm not sure what to expect.

"What's the matter?" he asks, not even touching me yet.

My face is red and his face is hovering right above my pussy. "I'm nervous. I haven't had…that before."

At that he grins. "Fuck, I love I get to show you." He wraps his arms around my thighs. "Hold the fuck on, baby. Your life is going to change."

His drops his head, his tongue gliding across my clit.

"God!" I yell, not expecting it to feel like that. I grip the sheets. I'm so sensitive. He was not wrong; my life has changed.

I close my eyes, feeling everything. My legs are shaking, I've lost all control of them, my toes curl.

The sound he's making makes me think that he's enjoying this as much as me, like he's the one getting pleasured and not me.

I can't wait to do this to him. I want to watch him fall apart and know that I caused him to do that.

A finger slowly glides into me. I clench around his finger hard, wanting to drag him deeper inside of me.

Another finger joins and he curls them up.

I scream, clenching around him hard as I come apart, orgasming so hard everything turns black around me.

I lose control of my whole body. All I know is the incredible pleasure I'm feeling between my legs.

He doesn't stop there. He keeps going until he wrings another orgasm out of me and another one until I'm not sure I'm even on this earth anymore.

After what seems like hours, he finally lets me breathe. He glides up my body with a cocky grin on his face. I don't even care about that, because the way he made me feel? He earned that.

"You have killed me," I joke.

He laughs, reaching between my legs, running his fingers over my clit. My hips jump off the bed from being so oversensitive.

"Are you okay going further?"

I nod. "I may kill you if you don't."

He gives me a wicked grin. "Try, darlin'." He takes my nipple in his mouth, nipping hard, causing a slight sting that shoots straight to my pussy.

"Let me grab a condom." He starts to move off the bed.

"Wait, I have an IUD, unless you want to wear one. I'm clean."

His hand wraps around my neck, putting slightly pressure

just to get my attention. "Good, I want to fill you up with me."

My eyes widen at his words. I lick my lips, wanting nothing more than to be filled with him. To feel his powerful body between my legs.

He spreads my legs, moving between me.

He takes my hands, intertwining our fingers together by my head. His face hovers above mine, eyes soft, full of tenderness.

"You ready, darlin'?" he asks.

I nod. "More than ready," I whisper.

Butterflies have filled my tummy to the brim, and my heart is beating so hard I am sure he can feel it.

He kisses me so deeply, I feel it everywhere.

He lets go of one of my hands, positioning himself before slowly sliding inside of me.

I wince before I can stop myself.

He stops completely. "I'm so sorry, baby. You're like a fucking vise."

I tighten my legs around him. "I'm okay, keep going."

He studies me for a second then reaches between our bodies to rub my clit.

"Ah!" I tilt my hips, moving him farther inside me. He takes over, filling me to the hilt.

"God, this is the best thing I've ever felt," I moan, throwing my head back. There is the bite of the pain, but the rest of straight pleasure.

He kisses my exposed neck, and his hand wrapped around my neck tightens enough to heighten my pleasure.

He starts to move, his face back in front of mine. He captures my hands again, and our eyes never break apart. Every touch, every little thing, we are feeling together—him inside of me, the way he is making love to me, filling a part of my heart that was broken so long ago.

He presses his forehead against mine and moves inside of

me so tenderly, gently, and the pleasure is so deep, slow, and burning.

We don't change the pace. Everything in this moment is unrushed. We don't want the moment to end.

"God, Konrad," I moan when he hits that spot from earlier that drove me crazy.

He's shaking, barely even able to control himself, and I lost myself long ago.

My body is not my own. It belongs to him completely.

His hand shoots down between our bodies, pinching my clit hard. I bite his shoulder so I don't scream as loud as I want to as I fall apart.

I clamp down so hard onto him, I'm sure he's in pain. He moans loudly into my ear, his movements fast, hard as he comes inside of me.

He falls on top of me. I wrap my arms and legs around him, holding him. He holds me just as tightly.

He lifts his head, looking at me. "Darlin', I will never be the same after that."

I laugh loudly, my voice hoarse from the noises I made. I'm almost embarrassed, but I won't be embarrassed by that.

I smile. "I am so happy, Konrad. You make me so happy," I admit, feeling vulnerable.

He kisses me. "Darlin', I am so much more than happy. I've waited for you my whole entire life."

God, I shake my head at the heady feeling that overwhelms me. I almost don't know how to react to it all.

He slowly slides out of me and walks into the bathroom, where he wets a washcloth and walks back to me.

What is he doing?

He spreads my legs, cleaning me.

It takes my breath away, my lips trembling from such tenderness from him and the way he is taking care of me.

He tosses the washcloth into the laundry basket and slides into bed with me again, pulling me until I'm lying on his chest.

"Are you feeling okay?" He rubs my back gently, and goosebumps break out across my skin.

I nod against his chest before looking up at him. I am happy, incredibly so. "I'm more than okay."

He smiles, cupping my face and pressing a sweet kiss to my forehead. I feel complete and utter peace right now.

I snuggle deeper into his chest, closing my eyes. For the first time in my life I feel completely, utterly safe.

9

TWO WEEKS LATER

I WAKE up slowly to a hand running across my back. I grin into my pillow before I look up to see Konrad lying beside me, shirtless, the happiest, most content smile on his face.

"Good morning, darlin'." His voice is deep, husky from his sleep.

I stretch my arms above my head, the smell of the ocean soothing me. Yesterday he packed my bag, put us on a private plane and whisked me away.

"Good morning."

There is a knock at the door. I sit up, pulling the blanket up to cover myself. Konrad bends over and puts on a pair of shorts. I can't help but tilt my head to the side to get a better view.

Konrad peeks back at me, grinning. He knows exactly what he's doing. I lie back on the bed, closing my eyes for a second.

I've never been on vacation before. I just felt like I haven't had time. Every time I had time to get away, another girl seemed to be in trouble.

Konrad handed my phone off to Shaylin, then kidnapped me and brought me here. The door slams shut and I jump.

"Sorry, baby."

I have issues with loud noises. If I'm prepared for it, it's not a problem, but if it's in a relaxed setting then it bothers me. PTSD is hard, but you learn to live with it.

Konrad settles into bed, putting the tray in front of us. "This looks amazing." I kiss his cheek, taking a bite of a piece of bacon.

"Darlin', nothing"—he winks—"I repeat *nothing* tastes better or looks better than you." His eyes slowly drift down my body, stopping at my pussy, eyebrow arched.

My face burns. "Stop!" I moan, covering my face.

He laughs loudly, prying my hands away from my face in amusement. "Darlin', how many times have I eaten your pussy in the last two weeks and you're still embarrassed?"

My face burns even worse at his words. He cups my face and squishes my cheeks. "You're so adorable, how can I not eat you up?" His voice is deeper, and his face shows his desire for me.

He kisses me, gripping the back of my neck, his thumb resting on my jawbone. My eyes flutter closed. His lips make love to my own. The sensation is toe-curling.

My hand falls to his thigh, rubbing farther and farther up until I cup him through his shorts.

He breaks the kiss, grabbing my hand and stopping my movement. "Oh, someone's being naughty." He kisses my cheek, rubbing my inner thighs enough to drive me crazy, stopping right before he touches me.

His finger rubs across my clit suddenly, and I almost fall off the bed. He catches me and continues slowly rubbing in circles.

My eyes roll back and I grip the blankets.

He kisses my shoulder. I throw my head back against the headboard and lie back.

His fingers are like magic and I'm still sensitive from last night. His lips suck my nipple deep into his mouth.

I reach down to hold his hand to keep from touching me as it's too much, but he grips it with his free hand.

My hips pull away and I bite my lip, screaming as I come hard.

My body relaxes. I try to catch my breath after all of that. His hands go under my arms, lifting me up so I'm sitting again. I put the tray over my legs while I'm in a complete daze.

"Eat." He points to the food, but I don't look at it.

The fingers that were just inside of me enter his mouth and he sucks them clean. Oh my God, did he just do that?

I turn my face down so he can't see my red cheeks.

He laughs again. "Darlin', you're fucking cute. Eat your damn food." He picks up another piece of bacon, making sure I take a bite.

"I wonder if I can fuck the blush out of you." He gives me a wicked grin before taking a drink of orange juice.

I shrug my shoulder. "You can try."

The look on his face lets me know that he for sure plans on doing that.

THE BEAUTIFUL WATER, the warm sand—this is heaven. I'm sad that I never experienced this before, but I'm so happy that I get to experience this with Konrad. He's in the water trying to surf and failing horribly at it. I've tried not to laugh, but it's hilarious because he's good at everything.

I look at the little girl playing in the sand directly in front of me with her parents, and my heart warms at the sight.

Konrad gets out of the ocean, water dripping down his washboard abs, his hair pushed out of his face.

God, I don't think there's a more beautiful man than him.

"God, will you look at that?" one of the girls behind me

whispers way too loudly. I laugh to myself at their comment, because he is beautiful and there is no hiding that.

But he is all mine.

I pull down my glasses, watching as he gets closer. "Oh my God, he's coming over." I can hear them scrambling behind me.

"Hi baby." He bends down and kisses me on the lips before lying down beside me.

"You did great surfing, baby," I tell him while rubbing his arm.

He gives me a look that tells me he knows I'm full of it. "It's a bad day for surfing is all."

I peek over to the guy surfing with no problem. He follows my gaze and picks me up off of the sand, throwing me over his shoulder. "I'm going to use you as a surfboard," he jokes.

I laugh and look back at the girls making comments. Their eyes are wide as they look at both of us.

Konrad carries me into the water, pulling me down until my legs are wrapped around him.

"I think I may just keep you here. I love seeing you on the beach. Later I have a spa day planned with you. You need to relax and have time to yourself. Let me take care of you like you do others."

I close my eyes, his words deeply affecting me. I wrap my arms around his neck and tuck my face in, breathing in his scent.

The waves move around us. It's quiet and in this moment it's perfect. He brings us deeper into the water, still holding me.

I sit up, my arms on his shoulders still. "I don't care where I am, as long as I'm with you, Konrad."

His head drops. "Fuck, baby, you know how to hit a man right in his heart."

Wait, his heart?

My stomach flips. With trembling fingers I touch the side of his neck. "Your heart?" I repeat his words.

The sun is starting to set but the air is still warm. "Yes, angel, my heart. I belong to you."

I rest my forehead against his. "I made a promise to myself years ago that I would not belong to another man." I lift my head, looking him in the eyes, wanting him to feel the gravity of my words. "But with you? All of me belongs to you. I never wanted to be anyone until you. You make me feel so safe."

He stares at me in awe, like he can't believe I'm saying what I'm saying to him right now.

His hands run under my butt, squeezing. "I need to fuck you right now," he growls.

I laugh as he runs out of the water with me in his arms. He sets me onto the towel and practically throws everything into our beach bag.

I can feel the eyes of the girls on us as they watch us gather our things. Konrad takes my hand and pulls me off the beach and into our house directly on the beach.

He lays me straight onto the bed, his eyes feasting on me. "God, to think this is mine."

He tears my bathing suit off of my body, literally. He picked it out. He bought me a whole beach wardrobe himself.

His hands drag up my body from my ankles to my inner thighs. His finger slides along my clit. "When we get home, I'm putting my cut on you. I need to see you in my cut with nothing on but that."

He falls to his knees, gripping my thighs as he goes down, sliding me to the edge of the bed.

"Shit, I just need a fucking chair. I could do this for days."

He walks across the room and grabs a chair, sitting in front of me. "Oh my God, are you really doing that?" I laugh at him being so ridiculous.

He grins wickedly. "Baby, I'm being serious. Sit your ass back and let me take care of you."

I fall back, letting him do whatever he wants to me. "How

long are you planning?" I stop talking at the first touch of his tongue dragging along my inner thighs.

My hands shake as I touch the back of his head. He looks up, licking his lips, sliding a finger inside of me oh so slowly. I clench hard around his finger.

"Whenever I fucking say."

I shiver at his demanding tone. "Yes, sir," I moan.

He gathers my hands, holding them together. "Do not move, you understand?"

My lips tremble at his tone. I am so overworked with need at this point. "Yes," I say breathlessly.

He winks and ducks his head. I try not to move. Every part of me is yearning to move, be closer, more, more, more.

Seconds later I'm coming hard against his face, my toes curled, my hands tight on his.

"That's one."

His rests his head on my thigh, his fingers doing the work this time. "Fuck, fuck, fuck!" I scream, still coming from the first orgasm when I come again.

An hour later I'm almost dead. I have died and come back to life a few times in this short period of time.

"I can't take it anymore." I finally push his face and hands away, scooting up the bed.

Konrad laughs, leaning back in his chair, arms behind his head. He lifts his hand that was just in my pussy a second ago to his mouth, licking it clean.

Oh my God. Goosebumps break out across my arms and legs. "Rest for a second, baby. I had to taste you. Now it's time to take you."

His eyes look me up and down, just staring so intensely like he's trying to memorize every part of me.

I'm shaking in anticipation of what he has planned for me next. This is the best torture—one I could deal with the rest of my life.

KONRAD

He stands up, taking off his shorts as he does so, leaving himself completely naked in front of me.

His hand wraps around his cock, stroking it from root to tip. I crawl to the edge of the bed. I open my mouth for him, and his hand moves through my hair, fisting it slightly.

"Is my baby hungry now?"

His hand moves from my hair to under my chin, gripping my face. "I'll let you have a little taste, baby." His voice is so deep, husky.

I'm dripping onto the bed. I can feel it dripping down my legs. I'm so turned on.

I take the head in my mouth, sucking on the tip, looking up at him. I don't touch him. My hands remain on the bed beside me.

He throws his head back.

I've never felt so powerful as I do right now knowing that with just my mouth I can cause him to lose his mind.

I take him as far as I can, gagging as I try to take him deeper. Konrad pulls back. "Don't push yourself, baby," he moans, moving his hips, slowly moving inside of my mouth.

I put my hands on his thighs, letting him take over.

He pulls out of my mouth, moving me over until I'm on my belly with my legs stretched out behind me.

His large thighs move on either side of my legs, his large hands gripping my ass cheeks, squeezing. "Ready?" he asks.

He always asks to make sure I'm okay. I nod. "God, yeah."

He grips my hands, lifting them above my head as he leans over my body. "God, sliding inside of you is like coming home." He enters me slowly. He's huge, so he has to give me time to adjust to him.

My eyes roll back in my head at the feeling of being so full, so much of everything.

He kisses the side of my neck, my shoulder. This is pure heaven.

"Faster."

"You got it, baby." He kisses my cheek before sitting up, pumping inside of me harder and harder until I can't even breathe. All I know is him, all I feel is him and nothing else matters.

I love him so much.

He stops and turns me around so I'm facing him. He intertwines our fingers by my head, kissing my neck.

We've fucked many times, but this? This is pure passion. I can feel his love for me.

His lips press against mine, slowly, gently, and I fall apart. I cry out. His mouth swallows my cries as he comes inside of me.

He's shaking as hard as I am, his arms unable to hold him up anymore and he falls beside me, holding me.

"Fuck," he groans.

I laugh, because that is exactly how I feel.

He grins wickedly, kissing my cheek. "Let's go shower before your spa day. Then I'm taking you out on the town."

He smacks my ass as he scoots out of the bed, taking me with him. My legs aren't cooperating yet.

"I can't move," I moan.

He laughs, stepping inside of the shower. The cold water sprays against his back until it warms and he moves me under it.

I kiss him sweetly, resting my forehead against him, the water rushing over the both of us. "I do love you." I grip his face, my heart so full. "You literally mean everything to me, Konrad. I just can't imagine a life without you."

His eyes are heavy. He's looking at me right now like his world revolves around me. "God, I love you too. The second I saw you, I couldn't bear to be away from you, baby."

He stands, holding me, both of us not saying anything but just in our feelings right now.

KONRAD

WE HAD dinner and now we're in a night club—another first for me. I'm in a dress that he picked out for me.

It's red, tight, backless, and I'm wearing black heels. My hair and makeup are professionally done.

I could get used to this.

I'm self-conscious of the scars on my back and the backs of my legs though. My dad used to hit us with a belt and the buckle sometimes left scars, and over the years they accumulated.

The look on Konrad's face made my fears dissipate. His hand on my back let me know that he doesn't mind.

He walks to the bar and orders me a fruity drink and a beer for himself. We take a seat. He pulls my chair closer to him, his hand on my leg. "Every eye is on you," he informs me.

I look around the club and I see quite a few eyes on me actually. I sip my drink and try to ignore the looks.

Konrad rubs my legs, trying to soothe me. I'm not comfortable with male attention, unless it's Konrad of course.

I finish my drink and set my glass on the table. "Want to dance?" I ask.

He finishes off his beer and walks me to the dance floor. He spins me around until my back is pressed against his front, his hands on my hips.

I lift my arm ups, behind his head. He moves my hips with his hands and soon we are lost in the music.

My eyes are closed and I'm just enjoying the moment. He kisses the side of my neck, his teeth nipping my ear.

I spin around to face him, kissing him. His arm bands around my waist, the other on my face.

A hand touches my calf, gliding up to my knee and inner thigh. It takes me a second to realize that it's not Konrad.

I spin around, gasping in shock that someone is touching me

like that, and much to my horror it's the girl from earlier from the beach.

"What the hell are you doing?" I ask her, shocked.

She grins at me then at Konrad and shrugs her shoulders. "What can I say? You are beautiful." She steps forward again, trying to grab me through my dress.

Konrad grabs her hand before she can touch me, pushing her hand back at her. "Don't fucking touch her, female or not. I don't tolerate that shit." I put my hand on his back, shocked.

She laughs at him, then her friends join in and I notice that they were on the beach earlier also. "What, is she that stuck-up of a bitch that she can't have fun?"

I jolt in shock at what she's saying about me. I step from behind Konrad as the shock wears off.

"Sweetheart, I'm not sure where you're from, but you don't touch someone without their permission unless you want your hand broke," I say casually, giving her the sweetest smile I can muster.

She looks at me in shock like she didn't think I was going to say anything back. She steps toward me.

I have fought grown men; she will be nothing. "Do it then, bitch," she hisses and lifts her hand, moving to hit me.

I catch her hand before it even hits my face. "Big mistake." I twist her wrist until she's on her knees in front of me. "Apologize and I won't break it."

She shakes her head no, her face red and tears in her eyes, but I don't have any mercy for her at this point.

"Get her!" she screams.

All at once, all of her friends jump me. Before they can touch me, Konrad steps in front of me, pushing all of them on their asses.

"Listen, I don't hit women but I sure as fuck will not be liable for my actions if you hurt her." His voice is scary. Right now Konrad is in a different place.

KONRAD

He puts his hand behind him, pulling me to his back, keeping me in place. I know that he let me fight my battles until this point and he has taken over.

One by one they get up and disappear into the crowd.

Konrad turns around and faces me. "We need to leave." His arm is around me tightly, leading me through the crowd and out the door.

Once we step outside, the night air calms me a little, the sound of the music muffling as the door shuts.

"She was crazy," I tell him, shocked.

He shakes his head. "I thought I had to worry about men. Didn't expect fucking females like that."

But honestly, women probably get away with it more often than men, but in my eyes, touch me without my permission, I don't see gender, I see an enemy.

I hear something like someone is trying to run up behind me. Konrad and I turn around too late.

A hand wraps around in my hair, jerking me back and out of Konrad's arms. She was hiding behind a vehicle.

Then three more girls come into view, running toward me.

I get to my feet, tearing my hair loose, and punch her straight in the face. Her face jerks back in shock and she hits the ground on her ass.

I notice that the three girls haven't touched me. I look around and see Konrad has all three of them on the ground, their faces smooshed into the hard pavement.

"Stupid bitches, I wish you were fucking men," he growls, and I can't help but laugh. He lets them go and runs to me, swooping me off my feet and into the rental in a second.

They run up and hit the window. The nose of the girl I punched in the face is bleeding. Her eyes are wild, scary. I feel like something is wrong with her to have this much anger over absolutely nothing.

Konrad takes off driving. They jump out of the way before he can run over them and we drive for home.

"What the fuck is happening?" I ask Konrad. I've never experienced anything like that in my life.

He shakes his head in confusion. "I'm just as confused as you. Those chicks were crazy."

The drive home is short, my nerves getting the best of me once we are alone. Konrad walks over and picks me up out of the SUV and carries me inside of the house, setting me on the bed.

"Darlin', I'm so sorry she touched you." He kisses my forehead. I grip his hands with mine, shaking.

"I'm fine. She didn't get to touch me anywhere important thankfully."

He shakes his head. "Doesn't matter where, it shouldn't have happened." He helps me out of my dress and into one of his shirts.

I scoot up to the top of the bed, and he comes out of the bathroom with my makeup remover. "Let me." I close my eyes and let him take off all of my makeup.

"There." His fingers wrap around my chin. "Beautiful, darlin'." He kisses my lips softly.

I smile, feeling much better.

He places the bottle on the bedside counter and scoots into bed with me, cuddling me into his side. "Do you ever want kids?" I ask him.

He stills for a second. "I do, I've always wanted to be a dad."

I thought that there was something wrong with me for a long time, because I couldn't get pregnant, so I got checked and I was fine. I am thankful every day that I didn't get pregnant with Michael's baby.

"I've always wanted to be a mom," I confess, smiling at the thought of holding my precious baby someday.

He turns me over until he's leaning above me. "Darlin', is this a hint?" He smiles sweetly, his eyes bright.

"I have an IUD, but if I do have kids, I want them to be yours."

He grips my hand, putting it on his cheek. "We can get lots of practice in." He picks me up, spinning me around. I laugh loudly as he kisses me.

10

ETTA

The second we left Hawaii, I wanted to go back, but I also miss the girls and I know I have a shitload of work to catch up on and I've been worried about all of them.

Konrad brings our bags into my apartment, setting them onto the floor. I fall back onto the bed, exhausted from the long flight.

My phone rings on the bedside table. I lean over and grab it, putting it up to my ear.

"Hello, this is Etta," I answer.

I hear a sniffling over the phone and I snap to attention instantly at the sound. "I need help," she whispers so softly I can barely hear her.

I put the phone on speaker so Konrad can hear. "Where are you and what's your situation?" My adrenaline is pumping.

I hear a shuffling sound like she's scooting across a wooden floor. "He forgot his phone with me. I am under Mr. Thompson's house. He is a teacher at Campton High. Please hurry, he will be back. My name is Baylee."

Oh fuck!

KONRAD

Mr. Thompson is a teacher at the school where Randy is the school principal. This is not good.

"We will be there soon, sweetheart. Toss the phone out of reach and delete the history so he doesn't know you called. We will be right there," I urge her in case he does come back and catches her.

The phone goes dead. I run to my closet and get my gear along with Konrad's, who is on the phone with the guys.

We need to get there. My best guess is he's probably scared out of his mind considering what's going on with Randy.

I remember when Baylee went missing, but I didn't learn about it for months because they deemed her a runaway because she was in foster care, so there was nothing I could do.

"Brian and Butcher are going with us!" Konrad yells and I pull the bulletproof vest over my head.

Konrad slips his gear on and I hand him a gun while I check to make sure mine is loaded and ready to go.

Konrad gives me a look and I know what it means. "I will be safe and I will stand behind you." I kiss his cheek and rush out of the door, not wanting to waste a second.

Konrad gets in the driver's side and I get in the passenger's. The others will meet up with us on the way to Mr. Thompson's house.

Konrad holds my hand the whole drive. Both of us are quiet as we go through every single thing that can happen and go wrong.

I hope Mr. Thompson doesn't discover that she has his phone, because the consequences could be fatal for her.

Nine-one-one tells them to stay on the phone, they get caught and the anger and the fear they feel in getting caught makes people do stupid things and the outcome is never great.

If she is who she says she is, she has been missing for six months.

I can hear the bikes before I see them. Brian pulls up behind us, with Butcher right behind him just as the house comes into view.

My first thought is that it's in the middle of nowhere. There is no one in sight and no one can hear screams.

The house is completely dark. I grip my gun tighter and I ready myself for what's to come.

Konrad slams the SUV into park and Butcher immediately runs behind the house, leaving Brian with me and Konrad.

Konrad kicks in the door, Brian right behind him, and I bring up the rear. I hear a loud boom from the back of the house. I know it's Butcher breaking in the back.

The house is silent.

"She said under the house," I mention.

I push rugs up off the floor, looking for a way into the basement when I see a weird rug to the side of the living room.

I walk over and push the rug but it won't budge. That's when I notice it appears to be glued down.

I get on my knees and find a little handle to the side of the rug that does come up. "Help me lift."

Konrad grabs the handle, opening the hatch. That's when I hear a weird sound. Konrad walks down the ladder, looking at me as he goes.

My heart is racing, Brian is next and then me.

I have a really bad feeling.

The light comes on suddenly. Right in the middle of the room on a bed is Baylee. I know her from her pictures.

She is so pale. My guess is it's from not seeing the sun in such a long time. "Baylee, I'm Etta. We just spoke, honey," I tell her softly.

She looks at the guys behind me. I know she's scared out of her mind. I can see the panic on her face.

"Do you want us to go back upstairs?" Brian asks.

She nods and they do so, leaving us alone.

I look around the small room. There are no windows, it's

just brick. The guys had to bend over to stand up in here.

It's so cold, mold is crawling over the walls. Her bed is filthy and so is she. "Sweetheart, I am going to untie you and we are going to get you out of here," I whisper to her softly.

She nods, watching as I slowly get closer and closer, not wanting to make any sudden movements and scare her.

She smiles at me weirdly, then her hand comes out from under her pillow and I see a gun.

My heart stops.

BOOM

BOOM

BOOM

Then nothing.

Konrad

THE SOUND of the gun going off is something I will never forget. I can't even breathe as I jump inside of the hole.

The sight before me is straight from my nightmares.

Etta is lying on the ground and the one we came to help is standing above her with a gun.

I don't hesitate. I lift my gun. Baylee looks at me in horror, but the bullet has already left my gun and plates in the middle of her forehead.

She falls to the ground, dead.

I run to Etta and see she's covered in blood, the source of which is her head.

Panic unlike any I have ever felt before races through me. I pick her up and carry her out of that fucking hole and place her into the back of the SUV, which is basically set up like an ambulance.

"DRIVE ME TO THE FUCKING HOSPITAL!" I yell at Brian, who jumps in the driver's seat.

I turn on the light and take off Etta's bulletproof vest, making sure a bullet didn't break through.

The wound on her head is pouring. I push her hair to the side and I can see her skull.

I almost pass the fuck out. It grazed her.

I put some oxygen on her, applying pressure to her head wound to stop the bleeding.

My hands are shaking so fucking bad I'm not sure how I even manage it.

"How is she?" Brian asks.

"She was shot twice in the chest but her vest stopped it. She was shot in the head but it looks like it grazed her." My voice is fucking shaking, I can barely explain.

I am so fucking scared. The thought of losing her is more than I can bear.

She moans and opens her eyes, her hands going to her head. "What happened?" she groans as she tries to sit up.

"No, honey, lie still," I beg her.

She looks at me for a few seconds before I can see the shift. "Baylee was fake," she says in such a heartbroken tone, tears in her eyes. Her face and hair are covered in blood from the wound on her head.

I close my eyes because this is going to fuck with her. I can see the hospital lights in front of me before Brian slams the SUV to a stop.

He runs around and opens the back. I get out, carrying Etta into the hospital. Butcher is right behind us.

Brian yells for some doctors and nurses. I set her on a bed, reapplying pressure to her head wound.

Everyone swarms us at once, asking a million questions that I can't answer, my full attention on her.

They start to push her away and I grab the bed, stopping them. "I am fucking coming with you," I yell.

"Call security!" the doctor yells, trying to pull her away from me again.

"She is not leaving my sight. I don't give a fuck what you say. I want a new doctor," I tell the nurse next to me.

She looks unsure of what to do, and the doctor looks at me in disbelief.

He reaches into the bed, his hands under her arms, and tries to fucking lift her up out of the bed with her bleeding everywhere.

Etta looks at me panicked, reaching for me.

I snap into action.

Brian tears his hands free just as I punch the doctor as hard as I can in the face. He hits the ground and I stand in front of him. "You will get me another doctor or so help me God." I let the threat hang in the air.

One of the nurses runs off. I turn to Etta to check on her. She's holding on to my pants. "I'm right here," I reassure her.

I hear a shit ton of footsteps like someone is running when I see security. "Get that man, he attacked me!" the doctor yells from the ground.

They come straight to me. I push them back away from me. They take out their tasers.

I want to rip them apart, I am so fucking angry.

Brian takes a look at my face and moves in front of me. One more thing happens and I will blow the fuck up.

"If you value your life, you will leave," Brian tells them. They look at each other unsure of what to do before they reluctantly leave.

The door opens and Myra steps out. "What is going on here?"

The doctor perks up at the sound of Myra's voice. "This man attacked me." He points to me.

Myra steps over him and runs to us. "Let's get her in trauma bay one!" I follow her. "You're letting them go?" the doctor screams and gets off of the floor, running straight for Myra.

I'm going to have to kill this stupid fucker.

I grip him by his throat before he can reach Myra. "She is an ole lady to the Devil Souls MC and Etta is a Grim Sinners MC ole lady." I put my face right in front of his, looking right into his soul.

"I would love to fucking kill you." I smile, loving the extreme fear on his face. I flex my hands, and his eyes roll back as I choke him.

I open my hand and he falls to the ground, out.

I run to catch up with Myra. Butcher stays behind with the doctor. I know he's making sure he doesn't cause any more trouble.

I stand in the back of the room as they do scans to make sure Etta's head is okay. The minutes feel like hours and the hours feel like days.

Etta keeps looking to me at the side of the room to make sure I'm still here. Someone would have to fucking kill me to leave her.

Etta

KONRAD CARRIES me inside of his house. This is the first time I have ever been to his home, but I have a major concussion from where I fell after Baylee shot me and I had to get a shit ton of stitches from where the bullet grazed me from my temple to the back of my scalp.

It was scary.

I can't get the look on her face out of my head from when she pulled the gun. She was so happy with herself.

I was tricked and I know that I will never go on a mission again without being super cautious.

Konrad lays me down onto the bed. He hasn't left me one second since it all happened last night.

KONRAD

"I'm going to go start your shower, baby." He kisses my forehead, letting it linger for a few seconds.

I nod and close my eyes. I am so emotionally exhausted.

I fall asleep the minute Konrad leaves, and I open my eyes to Konrad picking me up once more.

"I love you," I murmur.

His arms tighten around me. "I love you more than life."

I smile, and he sets me on the counter, stripping me out of my blood-stained clothes and then himself.

He carries me into the shower. "Tilt your hair back," he says gently, putting me under the spray so I can wash the back of my hair away from the stitches which is still caked in blood.

I reach for the shampoo, but he takes it from me. "I will." He sets me down onto the floor, keeping a hand on me as he washes my hair gently and then deep conditions it.

I'm shaking, not from the cold but everything that has happened and I am so tired.

I just feel betrayed in a weird way.

Konrad washes my body. This time there is nothing sexual about it. It's just straight him taking care of me.

"You're breaking my heart, baby." He cups my cheek, kissing my forehead. I drop my eyes as I let the tears fall.

I was shot by someone who I came to save, someone that I never expected. Konrad turns off the water, carrying me to the counter and drying me off as I cry into his chest.

I feel so raw and exposed.

The pain on everyone's faces as they rushed to the ER to check on me—my brother and Trey were completely panicked.

I hate that I caused that with so much going on right now.

Konrad didn't want to take me to the compound because he demanded that I needed rest.

He dries me off and doesn't bother dressing me. The soft pillow has me moaning. I am so tired.

He pulls up the covers and climbs in beside me, tucking me

into his front. "I was so scared I lost you. I don't think I would have survived it. I would have followed you."

I swallow hard at his admission and lean back to kiss him. "I would want you to live."

He shakes his head. "How could I live without my life?"

That was so deep. "Baby," I whisper, turning around and putting my head on his chest right over his heart.

"I know," he answers.

Right now there are no words for how I feel. This connection is something different, something that is beyond us.

I close my eyes and fall asleep to the sound of his heart.

Konrad

I DON'T SLEEP for hours. I count every single breath. Every little movement startles me from any sort of sleep I can muster.

When I do sleep, it's filled with nightmares, the sight of her lying there, and for a split second I thought she was dead.

It's haunting me.

I turn over and pull her into me, breathing in her scent, my arm around her waist. She puts her hand on my arm. I know I woke her up.

"Baby, can't sleep?" she asks, looking at me with her beautiful eyes.

I touch her cheek, rubbing my thumb along her cheekbone. "Sweetheart, I'm fine."

She gives me a look letting me know that she knows I'm not telling the whole truth. "Let me rub your back. You need the rest, baby." I turn her over on her belly, rubbing my fingers along her back.

She sighs, and I smile into my pillow knowing she'll be out in a minute. "I love you," she whispers once more.

I kiss the back of her head. "I love you, darlin'."

11

KONRAD

A WEEK later

I have searched and searched for Mr. Thompson, but he has dropped off the face of the earth.

I look at the fucking cabin where I almost lost her.

The girl's body is still inside. I don't have an ounce of guilt for what happened to her.

Maverick is with me and we are staring at the house. "Ready?" he asks.

I nod, pushing the button. The house explodes instantly. I take satisfaction in the fact that he won't have a home to come to.

"How is Etta?" Maverick asks.

I smile at the memory of her getting ready tonight. "She's good. She's having a girls' night tonight with the ole ladies."

Maverick eyes widen. "Oh fuck, I forgot about that. Bell is going too."

I laugh. "I wonder what trouble they're getting into?"

Etta

"Go Lani!" I scream as she takes a shot. She swallows it down, shaking her head side to side from the burn.

Shaylin smacks her on the back, laughing at her expression of disgust. We're at one of the bars in Raleigh, Texas that one of the MCs own.

We have all of the Grim Sinners girls and the Devils, Adeline and Bell are watching over everyone with watchful eyes.

Jean was drunk when she walked in the door. She is an absolute nut and now she's lying over on the table.

"What is one thing you have always wanted to do?" I ask them.

Lynn is beside me taking everything in. She is shyer than most of the girls. Jean lifts her head, grinning. "I feel like busting some mailboxes and causing some hell." She lifts her arm like it's a baseball bat, swinging it.

"I do know of some houses in town that are cult members," I throw out, my brain kind of fuzzy from the alcohol and I really don't care if I fuck up their life.

Jean throws back another drink. "What are we waiting for!" she screams, turning in her seat and trying to hop down.

"Prospect, you are driving us!" I point to the one watching us. The guys may have let us have girls' night, but we are not without guards.

We're all in a huge-ass party bus that picked us up at home since there were so many of us.

We all file out of the bar, Adeline and Bell babying us all, making sure we can even walk outside, fixing our hair and clothes.

They are precious. They are the mom I never had. My mind wanders to my mother and if she is even alive, if she got remarried or what happened to her.

She didn't stop the abuse that we all suffered, but I also have a little sympathy for her because she married so young.

Maybe I'll make a trip to go see her?

KONRAD

Lynn sits beside me, taking in everyone. Lynn is quiet when she's around groups of people and that's why she's against the window, people watching.

"How is Michaela?" I ask.

She smiles widely. "Honestly she is doing great. She bounced back really well. Tristan is with her tonight for a movie night." Her smile gets even wider after she mentions Tristan. "Have you gone out a date yet?" I ask her. Her face reddens and she looks out of the window.

"We have one tomorrow night. I am so nervous, Etta," she admits, looking back at me, but I can see the happiness in her eyes, the kind of happiness she more than deserves.

I wrap my arm around her shoulders, hugging her. "I was nervous too around Konrad, but I took that chance and it's the best thing that ever happened to me."

She nods. "I trust him. He has been living with us since that night. We've become close; he makes me feel safe, Etta." She stops, her eyes misting a little from unshed tears. "I never expected to feel that."

My heart hurts that she has never experienced that before, but I also know how she feels. "I felt the exact same way. Enjoy the ride, sister. I know Tristan, and I know he will be good for you, but if he's not, I will cut off his dick." I leave the threat hanging.

River turns around and looks at us. She and Shaylin are sitting in front of us. "I will help, but Tristan is good."

Shaylin gets that crazy grin. "I'm always down to cause some pain." She pats her gun at her side.

One by one the girls on the bus throw out their agreement. Lynn looks at all of them and I know she is touched by their support.

Jean laughs hysterically in the front. "I think the guys should just let us take over the punishments." Then she stands up.

"WAIT, we need to get some toys!" she yells, pointing at a Walmart.

The prospect pulls in, letting us off at the door. Two of the prospects are with us in the back—and probably in hell from the talks everyone is having.

The second we walk through the doors, we get some wild looks. "Let's wiener their yards too," Amelia jokes, and we laugh at the prospect.

I jump up and down. "Let's get some toilet paper!"

We make the prospects push the buggy for us as we throw in random items, little sticks for the hot dog wieners, forks so we can fork their yard, a few baseball bats.

The more we pile into the buggy, the more the prospect sweats. I know that he's going to need a week off after this. I smack him on the shoulder. "Cheer up, buttercup!" I throw in some glitter and paint.

Once we have everything loaded into the bus, I stand to the front. "All of these houses are guys whose wives we have rescued and taken in. So let's have some fun." I grin, sitting in the front and giving the prospects directions.

When I say cults are everywhere, I mean they are everywhere and they are so hidden because they live in normal society like most people, but inside of the walls of their houses, it's not normal at all.

The first one comes into view. All of the lights are off, but a vehicle is home. "Turn off the lights," I urge the prospect and he turns to the side of the road.

We run off the bus, laughing at the top of our lungs. I start putting forks in the ground, with Adeline helping me, which makes it even better.

Shaylin opens his truck door, throwing in glitter everywhere. Kayla has the toilet paper and she and Amelia get busy throwing it all over the house and trees.

Jean walks straight to the mailbox with the baseball bat and sends it up the driveway. She stops and studies it before grinning to herself.

A light comes on inside of the house, and we all take off running, laughing so hard we can barely manage to do so.

Alisha falls face-first and snorts with laughter. We pick her up, dragging her to the bus. She can't even walk from laughing so hard.

The prospect takes off speeding, now laughing with us. Our faces are glued to the window, watching him walk outside and seeing what his front yard looks like.

"Next house!" Jean screams, still holding her bat.

The next house is literally right up the road. I am the first one out of the bus, throwing toilet paper over the house.

Joslyn is throwing nails under his truck and the driveway. I snort because that will be a bitch to get out.

Lani smears Vaseline across the windshield, then glitter on top of that, but the best part is everyone is completely silent.

Gracelyn has paint and is painting nasty words on his front door. She is the sweetest of us all and it makes me giggle.

I'm standing back watching everyone's back when a light comes in the house. "Gracelyn!" I yell and she takes off running off of the porch. I take her arm, along with Paisley, who is next to me, putting forks in the ground.

I pull both of them behind a bush, which is partially hidden behind a tree so we can stay covered.

The other girls made it onto the bus, but we were so far away from the others that we couldn't have made it back in time.

"What the fuck is this?" a man yells, and I almost fall to the ground at his voice.

It can't be. There is no way. I almost throw up, my heart pounding so hard in my chest.

Then a women's voice is next gasping. "Oh my God, who did this?"

Everything goes dark for a second. I can't breathe. I don't even think I can move, but I have to see. I have to see if this who I think it is.

I stand up, looking at the people on the porch. I go through so many emotions, but one thing is for certain—the people on the porch are not the old owners.

I am face to face with Michael, my ex-husband, and my mother, but they don't see me because I'm hidden by the tree.

My mother kisses his cheek and rubs his chest like she's trying to soothe him.

I almost throw up at the sight. And to think I had a bit of sympathy for her.

Paisley moves to stand up next to me. "What's wrong, Etta?" she whispers in my ear, taking my hand.

I shake my head from side to side in disbelief at what I am seeing.

"Come on honey, come make me feel better."

Paisley's head snaps around at the sound of my ex-husband's voice. My mother is wrapped around him like he's the best thing that ever happened to her.

I told her how he hurt me, forced me to do horrible things and the way he took great pleasure in everything that he did to me.

He hated me but loved to hurt me more than anything. She told me that it was the way married life is, that it does get better in time once I'm used to it and it's my job to pleasure him.

She said that to me and now she's here with him. Did they plan this?

"Mr. Thompson!" Paisley gasps, looking at Michael.

I practically fall to the fucking floor. I turn around, gripping her arm. "What the fuck are you saying?" I ask her.

"That is Mr. Thompson, one of my old teachers."

My head tries to wrap around what I just learned.

Oh fuck.

12

ETTA

THE SECOND THEY are back in the house, we sprint to the bus. I am so confused and hurt. My worst nightmare was right in front of me.

I can't believe that this is happening.

Lynn is standing at the door when we run in, looking just as horrified as I am because I know she saw who was there.

"Etta, I can't believe it." She is shaking her head side to side, just as floored as I am. I sit in the first seat I can find, trying not to have a panic attack.

"What the fuck is happening?" Shaylin asks.

"That was Etta's ex-husband and our mother together." I can hear the gasps from everyone, especially Lani.

Everyone knows my story and Lynn's. We have not been shy with what happened to us and our story because we have used it to help others.

Shaylin tears off of the bus first at a full fucking sprint, River right behind her. One by one they jump off the bus like their butts are on fire.

Lynn looks at me, confused, but we follow. Shaylin kicks in the front door without a second thought and the girls follow in.

Lynn grips my hand as we walk inside of the front door, and right on the couch is Michael, my mother on her knees in front of him.

He pushes her off and he takes in the sight of the group of girls in front of him until his eyes settle on me.

I am not the same eighteen-year-old girl who left him. His eyes widen when he takes me in before they turn mean—the same look I'm used to.

Shaylin steps in front of me. "Get them!" she yells and she charges straight for Michael, punching him square in the face.

River goes straight for my mother, dragging her by her hair along the floor before she starts beating the ever-loving shit out of her, tearing out her hair by the roots.

I can't do anything but watch this happen. Bell and Adeline are hugging me and Lynn.

He tried to kill me with the set-up. He is Mr. Thompson. That's how the principal got in with the cult.

Shaylin smashes his face into the coffee table. Kayla kicks him on the back at the same time.

Michael yells loudly before he stands up, pushing Shaylin off and onto her ass, but she quickly gets up. He looks at me dead in the face, his face showing his hatred for me. "I am going to come for you, Jezebel, watch your back." He backs away until he runs out of the door, one of the prospects on his ass to catch him.

He just threatened me. I knew he had it out for me, but hearing it, knowing it, is different.

He has been here under our noses all of this fucking time, right here!

My mother screams from the ground. "Don't leave me, baby!" she yells, like he's going to come back for her, but he doesn't. The prospect does come back and he doesn't return with Michael.

Amelia holds my hand. "I think it's time we call in the guys."

We all stand around in the house. I don't call Konrad—I have

Lynn do it for me because I know I will break down if I talk to him right now because he is my safe place.

The wait for them to show up is so long. I can't believe Michael was here. I have had nightmares so many times of coming face to face with him again.

Konrad

THE SECOND LYNN and not Etta called me, I knew something was horribly wrong. All I heard was the name Michael and I was out of the door.

I met up with the guys along the way. I was at the compound waiting for her to be brought back home.

Driving along the road, we see a house that is completely trashed and I shake my head, knowing that these girls are the reason for that.

I pull to a stop in front of the bus and I see all of the girls standing inside a small house.

I run up to the door, the guys on my ass, to see what the fuck is going on. Etta is standing closest to the door and she looks absolutely devastated.

Vinny stops dead in his tracks, looking at the woman on the ground. "Mom?" he says and Trey hisses, looking at Etta and Lynn, who are deathly pale.

Etta looks at me and then at the ground. That shit kills me. "We were trashing this house when they walked outside. It was Michael and my mom together. The girls ran in here and beat Michael." She stops, swallowing hard, looking down at the woman who gave birth to her. "He got away, he threatened me and said he will be back for me."

I can see the fear in her eyes, which she doesn't show often. "Angel." I slowly make my way to her and pull her to my chest, holding her tightly.

I can see that this has fucked with her. I pull her head back, smoothing her hair out of her face. "I love you, baby. You are safe with me, always." I kiss her forehead. She closes her eyes and I can feel her physically relax in my arms.

Lynn sniffs beside me, staring at her mom. I pull her to me too and tuck both girls in my arms.

Their mom is crying on the floor, not crying for her life but crying for Michael who left her.

I shake my head at the disgusting display.

Tristan runs in the door and Lynn jumps at the sight. "Who has Michaela?" she asks.

He pulls her straight to him, holding her tight. "My dad is with her. I came for you."

I smile at the display and Trey scowls, but I think he just lost another one. Shaylin drags up their mother by her hair and onto her knees so she is facing the room.

She looks at Etta and Lynn. I want to rip her fucking eyes out of her sockets. How fucking dare she? She is disgusting for the way she has treated her kids.

"Etta, don't let them kill me," she pleads, holding her hands up like she's begging her.

Etta steps out of my arms, going to her mother. She grips her face, hard, pulling it up until she is looking up at her. "You do not speak to me. I could kill you myself but I won't. That's going to be left up to someone else. You are nothing, you are a piece of shit who only cared about herself."

I am so proud of her. She does not flinch. Her words are true and I know she means every bit of it.

She pulls herself from Etta's grip, glaring at her. "How dare you speak to me this way! I am your mother and you will help me!" she screeches before she turns her eyes to Lynn. "My sweet daughter, come help me please. I was good to you."

Lynn shakes her head no. "You married me when I was fourteen years old to a man that was over twice my age. You are not

KONRAD

my mother. You let others hurt me, didn't protect me. You gave birth to me, but that's it."

She looks to Etta again. That's all it takes for me.

I step up to her, gripping her by her hair hard. "You will not look to her again or I will rip your eyes from their sockets and make you eat them. Do you understand me?" I growl at her. I have so much anger, it's taking everything in me not to follow through on my threat.

I let her go and she falls to the ground crying. "Please, Vinny, help your momma. I beg you, son."

Lani takes over. "You do not speak to him either. You think I don't know what you have done, bitch? Did you know she loved when her kids were hurt and she watched it happen?" Lani tells the room, her face red with anger.

Etta closes her eyes and Lynn looks to the ground, giving me all of the confirmation I needed.

"Shaylin, you can handle this?" I ask. She doesn't deserve to live her life anymore.

We hear a sharp cry from the back of the house. We all look at each other in shock because it sounds like a small baby.

Etta runs to the back of the house. I follow her with Lynn. She pushes open a bedroom door and right in the crib is a newborn baby.

Fuck me.

Lynn pushes her way through and reaches inside of the crib for the baby. My first thought is, he doesn't look great. The diaper he's wearing is so old that it's hanging to his feet.

Tristan starts rummaging through the drawers and gets out a diaper. Together the both of them work to get him taken care of.

Etta puts her arm around my back and Lynn snuggles the now clean baby. We walk back into the living room.

"Well you found him," their mom deadpans like it's no big deal.

Lynn is angry. "He's in horrible shape, he hasn't been bathed and he hasn't been properly fed. How could you do this?"

She shrugs her shoulders. "I didn't want him, I wasn't going to let him starve. I raised you guys. I didn't have help. That's why I was here—to get Michael to help me raise him."

She looks to Etta like it's all her fault her plans didn't follow through. Lynn looks at me then at the baby. "I will raise him as my own. He's my brother."

"I will help you, anytime." Etta walks to her and stares down at him. Vinny joins them and takes him from Lynn. "I guess we have a baby brother. We'll do it together."

"Well, isn't this beautiful. You're taking my son from me!" Etta's mother screeches and tries to get up.

Shaylin punches her in the mouth. "Why don't you shut the fuck up? You're ruining the moment, bitch. "

I am ready to get out of here, take Etta now and get away from her. "Shaylin, can you handle this?" I know this is a lot to ask her.

Amelia and Chrystal step up. "We will take care of it. Get them home," Chrystal says and Tristan helps Lynn with the baby and I help Etta.

As they both walk out and don't look back, we can hear screams coming from the house.

13

ETTA

A MONTH Later

My eyes are closed as the warm Texas air flows through my hair on the way to his parents' house.

I'm finally meeting them.

I'm terrified out of my mind. I'm so scared that they won't like me, but I want to meet the people who raised such an amazing son.

The journey to their house is absolutely beautiful. It's very rural and has small-town vibes.

An hour from his house, we pull up a huge driveway with a gate at the front.

As we drive along the driveway, we see horses running with us, cows on the other side, and then a beautiful wooden home with a matching barn slowly comes into view on top of a slight hill.

"Wow, it's so beautiful here," I tell Konrad.

He nods his head and a woman walks outside in a pair of jeans and a button-up shirt. She looks to be in her sixties.

The second he stops the bike, she is hurrying off of the

porch and to him. "My baby is home." She starts kissing his face and I have to laugh at his squirming.

It makes me happy that he had such a happy childhood. The door opens and a man that looks like Konrad walks outside and smirks when he sees his wife. "Darlin', I think you need to leave my boy alone."

I know right off the bat where Konrad got the name *darlin'* from. I smile at the both of them when their eyes turn to me.

Konrad helps me off the bike and puts me in front of them. "It's so nice to meet you both," I tell them honestly.

His mom Geraldine gives Konrad a soft look before she swarms me in a mother's hug, the same one that Bell and Adeline give—the best hug; it's warm and feels like home. She pulls back and cups my cheeks. "It's so nice to meet you, the woman who has captured my son's heart."

My heart warms knowing that he has been speaking about me. "He has mine too," I admit, and she smiles warmly.

"That means grandbabies are soon!" she giggles, and his father pulls her back, but my mind is stuck on the idea of babies.

Am I against the idea of babies? Definitely not. I would love to have his babies.

I almost volunteered to take in Zane myself but I didn't know if Konrad would have been on board. Lynn and I are going to share him. I get him a few nights a week and he lives there.

"Come on, dinner is ready!" She waves us all in and his dad saddles up next to me and gives me a quick side hug. "Nice to have you here."

The nervousness is thrown out of the window knowing how nice they are. Konrad doesn't let go of my hand and pulls out my chair for me to sit down at the dinner table.

His mom has made a custom southern day meal with fried chicken, mashed potatoes, corn, green beans, the works.

KONRAD

"Wow, this looks absolutely amazing!" I tell her, and she looks at me like I'm her favorite person.

Konrad puts his hand on my thigh under the table, giving me a squeeze. He looks super happy and content right now.

"Alright, dig in, everyone." Konrad's mom motions for everyone to serve themselves since everything is laid out in front of us.

Konrad doesn't let me make my own plate, insisting on doing it for me, and I notice that Konrad's dad is doing the same thing for his mom. They're both sweet.

Me and his mom share a look. I can see the happiness on her face and I know I am experiencing the same kind of happiness.

"Etta, Konrad told me about the work you do. That's so amazing, but I imagine it's so tough," she tells me. I nod after I take a bite of food.

"It is tough. Konrad has been on every mission with me lately though." I smile at him, resting my head on his shoulder for a second.

He kisses my forehead and we eat together, his parents making small talk about how they met in high school and they've been in love ever since.

Once we eat, Konrad's mom takes my hand and leads me into the living room, and I notice there's a ton of photo albums on the coffee table.

I smirk at Konrad's horrified expression. "I have to show you Konrad when he was a baby."

She opens the first one—it's his first year book. I let her show me every little picture and I ooh and aww as I know this is very important to her.

"He loved to run around naked with no clothes on. He would have to pee and he would do it right in the store. He was crazy." She starts laughing and I join her. Konrad's face is red with embarrassment.

"Aww, you were just adorable." I tug on his hand so he can sit next to me on the couch and look at the photos with me.

"Do you have any photos of you when you were little?" his mom asks.

I shake my head no. "I don't have any. We didn't have a camera."

"Ohh, okay!" She goes back to showing me every single moment of Konrad's life until he was eighteen and joined the Navy.

"Then he was a SEAL. That was the scariest part of my life. I didn't sleep for years, but my boy is home and he's going to give me grandbabies."

I snort-laugh at her throwing in the grandbaby part at the end. Konrad rolls his eyes but laughs with me.

But she isn't laughing, she looks completely hopeful. "I may bring Zane over sometime."

She perks up at that. "Ohh, who's he?"

"He's my baby brother; he's two months old."

She gasps dramatically. "Can I please? We'll come and pick him up."

"Let me talk to my sister and we can work something out, no problem," I tell her. She wraps me in a tight hug like I just gave her the best gift.

It makes me happy that I can make her so happy. She is precious. She is the kind of mom I would want to be. She's a devoted mother to Konrad. She kept everything, even his first outfit and shoes.

"Mom, we better get going." She nods and hugs me then Konrad. "Let me know about Zane please."

I squeeze her hand one last time and climb on the back of Konrad's bike as his parents wave goodbye to us.

"Your mom is absolutely precious. I love her!"

He puts his hand on my leg. "She is pretty great."

The drive back is even more beautiful with the sun going

KONRAD

down. We decided to stay at his tonight since it's closer and I'm not needed at the compound right now. One of the guys is taking over the phone for me tonight.

I fall into Konrad's bed, groaning, tired. He laughs and pulls my shirt over my head and my jeans down my legs. "Let's go shower so we can sleep."

I slowly and tiredly make my way into the shower. Last night we had Zane and I think he missed Lynn because he was not a happy camper with us.

The second that Tristan and Lynn picked him up, he was content. Michaela is obsessed with Zane. She thinks he is a real-life baby doll for her to play with, but the great thing is, she's more than careful with him.

Konrad washes my hair for me. I don't even bother to try anymore. Since the night of the accident he has taken over and I can't fight him on it.

I close my eyes, loving the feeling of his fingers dragging across my scalp. I can't stop the moan that slips through.

He stops moving his fingers and grips my throat from behind. "The only time you moan like that is when I'm in you or my mouth is on you."

I shiver all the way down to my feet. His hands tighten on my throat, but the other hand snakes down my body to my pussy, his fingers sliding through my folds.

"Oh God," I moan again, and he rewards me by slipping two fingers inside of me. "You are drenched."

"Soaked."

He growls and plants my hands onto the shower wall, bending me over until my ass is up in the air.

I look back at him, loving the sight of him above me, huge and hard for me. I bite my lip, aching to be filled by him.

My eyes roll back in my head when he fills me to the brim, stopping when his hips touch mine.

I clench down on him hard, wanting him even deeper when it's physically impossible.

He wraps his arm around my stomach and the other on my hip as he pushes into me, hard.

I hold on as he lifts me up, bringing me even deeper, like I'm sitting on him. I moan deep as he moves harder, faster inside of me.

His finger digs into my clit, stroking it, and I shake so hard my feet move from under me, but he keeps me up, moving inside of me while holding me up. My eyes roll back into my head and I come hard.

He shakes just as hard as me as he fills me with his come. He slowly slips out of me and I lean my head against the wall, just trying to breathe.

He cleans me gently and carries me back into our bedroom, laying me down onto the bed.

Once we're settled, I turn on the TV and snuggle into his arms. "Have you thought about your mom's questions about babies?" My stomach is filled with butterflies, I'm so nervous.

He turns me over onto my back so he is looking down at me. "I would love to have babies with you. I didn't want you to be scared because it's sudden."

My heart sings with happiness that he wants the same thing I do. I smile widely. "I want to have your babies, Konrad."

He smiles back. "Alright then, let's get your IUD taken out tomorrow?"

I laugh at the suddenness, but I want that. I know that he's the one for me. There is no hesitation there.

He nods. "I'll go with you."

I kiss his cheek, happy that he is on board with me. His mom is going to be thrilled.

"Plus, it takes some people a long time to get pregnant," I point out, and he nods. "That's why I was thinking you can go tomorrow and I can get busy on that." He winks, kissing my cheek, snuggling me back into him.

The Next Day

I'M SITTING on a bed in a gown with Konrad at my head. It hurt really bad when they put in the IUD, but hopefully it won't be as bad getting it out.

The doctor comes in and I close my eyes, waiting and waiting, then she makes a weird sound.

Konrad is stroking my hand to keep me calm, but I look down at her. "I can't seem to find it."

My eyes widen in fear. "What do you mean you can't find it?" I ask her, confused and scared.

"Let's get you an ultrasound just to make sure it's not in there and we will go from there." The doctor smiles reassuringly.

I hold Konrad's hand tightly. The doctor gathers the ultrasound wand and I close my eyes. "Where is that going?" he asks, but shuts up when I squeeze his hand hard.

She looks at the screen and her eyes widen. I look at Konrad, worried. "Okay, I think your IUD has fallen out, because you're pregnant."

I almost fall off the table in shock. "You're around six weeks, if I had to guess. Congratulations."

We look at her like she's crazy, then it slowly starts to sink in that I have a baby inside of my belly.

I touch my stomach in disbelief before she turns on the sound of the heartbeat. I gasp at the beautiful sound.

Konrad puts his hand over mine on my stomach, our eyes glued to the screen. I'm happy, but I'm just shocked that it happened like this because it's so unexpected.

I don't even know how it fell out. I don't even remember it, but maybe it's God's will that it happened like this, defying odds.

"Alright, mom and dad, here are some prenatal vitamins and some pictures for you. Make another appointment at the front desk."

The doctor leaves me to get dressed. Konrad puts my pants on for me and I look down at the picture, happy. "We are going to have a baby," I whisper in shock.

He looks at the picture with me before laughing. "My mom had the right kind of juju."

I laugh at that because she did keep mentioning it. I kiss him softly and slip my shirt over my head. "You're going to have to be careful, baby, especially with your missions now."

I nod in agreement. "I can stay in the vehicle until the place is cleared, then I can come in once it's safe."

He cringes and I know that he doesn't even want me to do that. "I'll be safe and you will be with me," I tell him, knowing that will make him feel better. He knows I'm buttering him up.

We make the appointment and head next door for lunch at a little sub place.

"I think I need to get some nutritious food for you. You need to eat better and more often."

Oh goodness, here we go.

He starts making lists of things he thinks I will need and food that I need to get out of my diet, Googling everything.

I prop my head on my hand, loving this, loving seeing the excited look on his face and knowing that he is so happy about it.

I just know he is going to be an amazing dad and our baby will have an amazing life like he did.

"Let's go to the baby store right up the road, just to look."

"Okay, honey." I kiss his cheek and eat my sub. He keeps his eye on me the whole time, making sure I eat every bite.

Inside of the store, he goes over every single detail, looking at car seats, baby beds and debating which one is safest.

"Do you think we should get this bassinet? It's number one in safety." He points to it and reads over the manual.

"I think it's really nice."

We waves over a worker. "We'll take this and this," he says, motioning to a body pillow for pregnant ladies.

I am going to be spoiled and so is this baby. I hope it's a boy that looks like him. "Ready to go home?"

He's carrying the bassinet in his arms and I'm following behind him, and he lets down the back of his truck, setting it in there.

"I can't wait to put it together."

14

ETTA

Life at the compound is busier than ever. We have had a lot of girls join and some even showed up to the gate. That made me uneasy because they know of our location.

Maci is helping me in the kitchen, getting dinner ready for everyone. I can't get over how much she has changed and what time can do for someone. Same with Olivia—she is outside in the garden picking some green beans.

"How are you settling?" I ask Maci.

She grins. "Robert is doing great. Life is amazing here, and I'm so thankful for the life you have given us." She hugs me slightly.

I smile. "I'm so happy that I get to do this. If I didn't have my brothers to take me in when I was eighteen and Lynn was sixteen with a toddler, our lives would have been so different."

She nods, saddened. "Yeah, I am so thankful for them too. I think that I want to start going on missions with you. You don't need to do it alone anymore and you can use the help."

My heart sings with happiness at her volunteering, and it's perfect timing since I'm pregnant. "I'm pregnant. Don't tell anyone, but I was looking to have some help," I tell her.

KONRAD

Her eyes widen with happiness. "Oh my gosh, I am so excited for you and Konrad!" She wraps her arms around me, squeezing me tight.

I am so excited to be a mother. Seeing the bassinet Konrad put together in my apartment makes me want to put her or him in it so bad.

Konrad is out with the guys today at the club house and they're going out on a ride. He didn't want to leave me, but he still needs his friends.

Maci lets me go. "This baby will be so loved by everyone. He or she will be raised by a village."

My heart warms at her words. "You girls are so important to me, thank you." I hug her once more and she grins, going back to cleaning her dishes.

We can see out into the huge backyard where a ton of kids are playing, and I love to see everyone together, happy and enjoying their life.

"So Brian, huh?" I tease Maci, and she blushes furiously.

"I don't think he's interested in me like that."

I give her a look. "Honey, you are all he talks about every time I'm around him."

She looks at me in shock. "Wait, he really does?"

I nod, smiling. "He sure does. He is infatuated with you."

She looks down at the sink and smiles. I can tell she is happy. "He is a great guy. He's coming over for dinner tonight."

I laugh. "No, he is not interested at all," I joke, flicking her with the towel.

She scoffs before she busts out laughing, her face still red with embarrassment. Lynn walks into the kitchen and Michaela runs out of the door into the backyard to where all of the kids are playing.

"Hi, sis." I hug her and she walks to the stove. "How is baby Zane?"

Lynn smiles. "He's with Tristan. They're having a guys' day together." She has a blissful look on her face.

We look at the kid outside of the window laughing at seeing Michaela playing baseball with the guys and her arm is like a noodle, barely able to throw the ball. "I don't think softball will be her sport," Lynn jokes and we all laugh.

At the back of the property I see a few kids running from the trees. I walk out onto the porch to see if I can get a closer look at what is happening.

It's Robert.

Maci gasps and starts running toward him. I follow her, and Lynn calls Michaela to her.

When Robert reaches us, I can see the tears on his face. "They have Olivia! One girl came to the gate wanting in and Olivia let her in, but it was a bunch of men! They're coming!" he says so quick I can barely understand him.

As he finishes, a group of men walk through the woods, and front and center is Michael, his hand wrapped around Olivia's neck with a gun to her head.

They are dragging her along and she's crying. I know she is scared out of her mind and I know she was afraid she was going to be taken again.

That won't happen with me around. I will fight to the death for these girls.

I turn around to Lynn. "In the house. Call the guys." She takes Michaela and runs into the house.

Maci is standing next to me. "Robert, run now!" she urges him and he follows direction, running for the main house.

The men stop fifty or so feet in front of us. My mind goes over a hundred different things that could happen and go wrong.

At the back of the gate, I see twenty or thirty more guys show up from the tree line.

We are under attack.

"IN THE BUNKER!" I yell to all of the women, and they scramble, knowing exactly where to go.

We have bunkers built under the ground for the women to escape to under the house. They know where the entrances are and the men won't be able to get in.

We planned for this to happen.

Maci and I are standing in front of forty men, us against them, but I will face worse odds to save my girls.

"Michael, I see your face is healing nicely," I greet him, and he glares at me. I know that touched a nerve.

He tightens his grip on Olivia, causing her to wince. "Look, we are here to get what is ours. If we get that, then we leave and no one else has to get hurt, like this sweet girl here." He rubs his hand along Olivia's cheek.

He smiles at me, no it's not a smile. His face is twisted with pure evil. "She reminds me of you at that age. I can smell the fear on her." He puts his nose into the crook of her neck. "God, it even smells like you."

My heart is beating so fast. The fear I have for her right now is unreal. I smile, pretending. "If she reminds you so much of me, then why don't you have me?" I lift my arms to the side slightly, motioning with my fingers to come here.

His eyes widen at that. He is not expecting me to give myself up and he gets angry at that. I think he has lost his mind completely.

All of the guys behind him are looking around the yard trying to spot their wives. They will never find them.

I hope Lynn is hiding. "Maci, why don't you run?" I whisper to her, but she shakes her head no and takes my hand in hers. "I will not leave you or her."

I let out a deep breath. "Let her go, Michael. She didn't do anything."

He licks his lips, making a smacking sound. "But she is

female. She was born to make a man sin." He grips Olivia's face hard so she is looking directly at us.

Her eyes are killing me. God, this is all my fault. He came here for me. "But she does not belong to me. She is the wife of our leader." He pats her head like she is a small child. "I am here to take her back to him."

Oh fuck.

Maci takes in a sharp breath at the realization and so do I. This changes things and I know Michael may have been here for me but they are really here for Olivia.

Olivia is looking at me with pure fear at the mention of the leader. Fuck me. This is so, so bad.

This is more than bad. No wonder they sent so many fucking guys here today. I hope that I can just hold them off until the guys get here and then we can be okay.

I have my gun in the back of my pants and I will use it if it comes down to it. Maci is holding onto my hand so tight I'm afraid she is going to break it.

But I have to give her props right now. She is standing with me and facing down all of them and is not showing an ounce of fear.

"Take me instead. You all know you want me. I have taken all of your wives," I gloat and I look around the compound. This is all because of me and the guys in the MC backing me up.

I can see the change in them instantly. I can see the anger in them that I have taken their wives.

Legally they are not their wives, there are no marriage licenses, but in their eyes it doesn't matter.

I have what gave them power—they fed on causing them pain and hurting them.

They thrived on that and now I imagine their embarrassment knowing they couldn't keep their wives in check because they ran away and I took them.

I have had a huge bounty on my head for years now, since

the first year I started doing this because they think I am the devil reincarnate.

I have seen sermons about me posted online, how I'm going to be the ruin of the world and I'm going to be the end of mankind.

My pictures have been posted, but they are the ones from the day I was married and I know that Michael and my mother have faced hell in the church because of it.

"What did you do to Cindy?" he asks me, breaking me out of my thoughts.

It confuses me why he is asking about my mom considering he left her there to face everyone.

I look at him like he is stupid. "What do you think happened to her?" I ask.

He shakes his head like he's in disbelief. He loosens his grip on Olivia and I know to continue. "What are you saying!" he hisses at me, taking a step closer to me. Olivia falls to the side slightly.

I smirk.

He's shaking from head to toe, and his eyes are weird as fuck. "She was your mother, you wouldn't kill her!" he laughs, pointing a finger at me. "You almost got me."

I look at Maci and she gives me a look that tells me she's thinking the same thing I am—this is his last straw.

"I didn't say *I* killed her," I tell him in a tone that suggests that someone else finished the job.

He stills and looks at me with such murder in his eyes. "You are dead." He lets Olivia go, and as soon as he does so, a shot rings out, hitting Michael's hand.

He drops his gun and screams at the top of his lungs in pain. Olivia runs to Maci and Maci practically carries her into the compound, with me on their ass to make sure they get inside.

I can hear the men running for us. I swear I can feel their breath on the back of my neck.

I step inside of the house and slam the door, but it gets caught on Michael's foot. Maci and Olivia press against the door with me to try to get it shut.

"Fuck!" I yell, taking a running go to push the door. I know it has to be crushing his foot by the yelling, but he's not taking his foot back.

I can see the other guys running up going to help him and if they get to the door to help him, then it's over for us.

"Olivia, run!" I plead with her before they get inside of the house.

She shakes her head. "I won't leave you and Maci."

Just as they reach the door, Michael is looking at us through the window. I see him smirk at us thinking that he is going to win, but then his expression changes and he's looking at something behind us.

I look around and I see Ronny running through the house to us carrying a sniper rifle.

Olivia gasps when she sees him. He pulls up my shirt and grabs my pistol out of the back pocket of my pants. He walks to the door, pointing the pistol at Michael's foot and pulling the trigger.

Boom

Boom

Boom

Michael screams at the top of his lungs, falling back and clutching his foot. I slam the door shut, locking it and arming it, knowing it will be impossible for them to get in now.

I turn around and look at Ronny in shock. I can't believe he's here, and just sixteen years old at that. "What are you doing here?" I ask him.

He rolls his eyes at my motherly tone. Maverick and Bell are going to shit their pants. "I heard what was going on and I was closest, so I came here first."

He looks at Olivia, concerned. "You okay? He didn't hurt you, did he?"

Ronny is massive for sixteen—he is around six foot five and over two hundred pounds. He is a freaking pro at hockey already and probably the most beautiful kid I have ever seen with his green-blue eyes.

She shakes her head no. "It just scared me is all, thank you for saving me." She smiles sweetly at him.

I think a feather could push him over. "It's no big deal," he says simply, but we are interrupted by Michael running into the door, trying to break in.

"Come on, ladies. Let's get you to the safe room." Ronny motions for us to follow him, but I move Maci and Olivia in front of me. "You guys go on and I'm going to keep an eye on things."

Ronny nods. "I'll be back, but I would get dressed up if I was you," he says, like he's a grown man, and I shake my head at that. I remember when he was a little boy, but now he's bossing me around.

I run to one of the spare armory rooms on the bottom floor. I get on my bulletproof vest first and put my gun strap on.

I need to be ready for anything and I need to protect my baby in my stomach at all costs, along with these other ladies.

This is the worst-case scenario that I thought would never happen, but here we are. All of the drills we have done have come to this, but right now?

I am going to war.

Ronny walks into the armory and we look at each other. "Ready for this?" he asks and I nod, preparing my gun.

"Let's do this."

15

ETTA

They are banging on every single door of the house—the windows, everything, trying to find a way inside.

I run upstairs to the roof of the house with Ronny. I can maybe start picking them off one by one from up here.

I hear a loud noise by the gate where the others came through, and I almost fall to the floor at the sight of at least fifty more of the cult members running across the field, but they aren't coming straight to the main house, no.

They are running for the small cabins where all of the women live.

Fuck.

I take out my phone and I do a level five lockdown on every single cabin. I will get alerted if they manage to get inside.

I pray to God everyone is safe.

"We need to take them out." I point to the ones running to the cabins and Ronny nods in agreement. "I was thinking the same fucking thing."

I am hit once again that he is sixteen years old. I put my hand on his arm to get his attention. "You don't have to do this."

He stares at me deep in my eyes. "We protect our people."

That's all the answer he gives me before he sets up his sniper rifle and lies down into position.

I jump at the first sound of the bullet leaving the chamber and I see a body fall to the ground.

I join him on the ground and point my own gun at one of the guys. Boom. He falls to the ground clutching his stomach. I know he is a goner.

I see a gun flash in the light. I push Ronny's head down right before a bullet strikes the walls by where we are lying.

"How far out are the guys?" I ask Ronny while peeking over the wall.

"They were an hour out when I talked to Mom. They should be here any minute." I look back into my scope, taking another shot. All of the men are still trying to make their way in the house below.

I can hear Michael trying to give orders and get help breaking in the front door, but it's almost impossible for it to be broken into.

I hear bullets hitting the glass. I wince at that but it's bullet-proof, thankfully, but it won't hold forever.

I pull my phone and I see texts from Lynn. "There is one in the house. He's locked in."

Oh fuck!

I show the text to Ronny and he starts to get up. "You're better at this than me. I will handle this."

I pick up my gun and run through the door. I let myself calm and I push the button to turn off all of the lights so he can't see.

I pick up my phone and I search the cameras, trying to see if I can spot the person in the house.

"What room are you in?" I ask Lynn through text.

"He's on the second floor, three doors from Sheryl's."

I hit the stairs, running as fast as I can to make it down. Lynn is different than me. She is not a fighter like I am.

I look into the scope, detecting thermal, and I can see him at the end of the hallway.

Fuck, he is right outside of where Lynn is hiding. Why didn't she get into a safe room?

I make sure I don't make a sound as I approach, then I hear a loud bang and the sound of Michaela screaming.

The not-making-a-sound idea goes right out of the window. I walk inside of the bedroom and see he is trying to break down the closet door.

I see red at the sight of him trying to get inside to them. I lean against the door casually. "Well, well, how did you get in here?" I smirk when I see it's my brother-in-law, Michael's brother.

He spins around to look at me and I use my phone to turn on the lights once more. I want him to see who it is when I beat his ass.

He looks me up and down. "You're alone?" He looks behind me like someone is magically going to appear behind me.

"I am." I look to the closet and I can hear Michaela crying inside.

"Look, I just need Michaela and then I will leave. That is all," he says so simply, like it's nothing.

I laugh. "You think I will give up my niece?" I point my gun at him, right at his dick. "I will never fucking give her up, you stupid piece of shit!" I scream and start to pull the trigger, but another gun goes off behind me.

He hits the ground, holding his dick in his hands like that is going to save him. I whip around and see Konrad standing in front of me, decked out head to toe in gear. He has a hat on backwards and is brandishing an AK.

Relief floods through me. His mask drops and he rushes to me, pulling me to his chest, holding onto me so tight. "God, I was so scared, baby," he whispers into my ear. I can feel him shaking.

"We are safe. Ronny saved Olivia." I tell him how it all went down, and he has a proud smile on his face at the mention of Ronny. "I love that fucking kid."

I hear a loud boom and glass shattering, letting me know that they have made it inside of the house.

Shit!

"Lynn, open the door. We need to move, now!" Konrad yells through the door and she opens it immediately.

He reaches down and scoops Michaela into his arms just as Tristan thunders his way into the room. He has a wild look in his eyes and blood on his shirt that lets me know that he fought his way in.

"One hundred more just flooded through the back gate. We need to move." Tristan takes Michaela from Konrad.

Konrad nods, the mask slipping back into place. We have been attacked and we didn't expect this to happen like this.

Tristan hands Lynn Michaela. "You need to hold her. I will get you guys out of here," he promises her.

I help her situate Michaela and I lift my gun, ready. I nod to Konrad, letting him know that we are ready.

"We need to take them to one of the guest houses and into the ground," Tristan says, and I agree immediately.

"Wait, Maci and Olivia are inside here!" I forgot that they ran through the house trying to find safety.

I look at the motion detector on my phone and see that they slipped through a room right down the hallway.

"They are right down here!" I whisper-yell, just as I hear someone running up the stairs. Konrad steps in front of me, shooting them the second they make the first step onto the landing.

"Michael is mine when I find him," Konrad tells us. I can feel the darkness inside of him.

I look down at Michaela to see if she is okay, but Lynn has her face covered so she can't see what is happening.

We make our way down the hallway to the room where Maci and Olivia are. "You guys, we need to run!" I yell into the room and they pop out of the bathroom instantly. I know they were listening to see if anyone was coming.

Olivia runs to me. I take her hand. "Hold onto to me and don't let go," I tell her and she nods. I can see the fire in her eyes.

Huge-ass footsteps break the moment and I hold my breath, waiting to see who the person is. Tristan is in the back of the group and he fires off one single shot, the bullet hitting the person directly in the face.

"Let's move." Konrad takes the head and we go down a back stairway to the first floor.

My adrenaline is running so high right now, anyone could cross in front of us at any second.

I can hear gunshot after gunshot outside and inside. I hope that Michaela won't be affected by this. That would be my worst fear.

Konrad stops suddenly before he is tackled to the side by someone. I watch in horror as the guy brandishes a knife, trying to stab Konrad in the side.

Konrad pushes him off. My stomach twists with the urge to throw up at the extreme fear I am feeling.

Konrad lifts his gun simply and just shoots him point blank. "I don't have fucking time for this shit."

The knife hits the ground first as he clutches his neck where Konrad shot him, blood hitting the floor.

The clean-up is going to take fucking forever here. Why that crossed my mind, I have no clue.

We step outside onto the porch and I see bodies on top of bodies lying on the ground, but more people are running everywhere.

This is a mess.

I hear a gunshot from the top of the house and I know it's

Ronny. Maverick runs past us with two pistols, with Smiley at his back. "Where is Ronny?" Maverick asks me.

I point to the roof just as another shot rings through. Maverick shakes his head, grinning as the body hits the ground. "My boy is too good of a shot for his own fucking good."

Olivia steps forward, her face serious. "He saved my life. He saved me from getting taken." Her body is shaking so hard from the adrenaline, the fear, and so much more.

Maverick's face changes at the realization and I know what Ronny did is sinking in. "Let us help you take them to safety," Maverick tells Smiley and us.

They move on either side of us, putting us in the middle of a barrier, which is them. Maverick looks at me and smiles, arching an eyebrow to check if I am okay.

I am.

Seeing Michael this time didn't shock me, no. I was prepared for it and this time it was different. Lives were in danger.

"There is a cabin right through those woods." I point and we all move as one unit. I peek back at Lynn and Michaela to make sure they're okay. Lynn is carrying her with her eyes covered so she doesn't see the bodies lying around.

Tristan has his hand on her back like he is trying to reassure her that he's there and she's safe.

This is horrible. We're coming around the side of the house and we're going to be out in the open, but we have no choice considering that's how we can get to the cabins.

Konrad peers around the corner to make sure it's clear, his arm lifted, and he waves us forward with him.

The second we get ten feet from the main house, five guys come around the front of the house and we are fucked.

One of the guys yells out, "Here she is!" and points at Olivia. She looks pale and shaken, because every single guy is looking at her like she is the last meal on earth.

Fuck me.

One of them starts running toward us, and before I can lift my gun, a shot rings out and he doesn't make it five feet before he is dead.

I look up to the roof at Ronny and he's grinning from ear to ear. "My fucking kid," Maverick laughs as Ronny makes the rest of the guys scatter back to the front of the house.

We take their moment of distraction and run for the cabin. Konrad opens the door and we all four run inside. I push the button on the wall, opening the hole in the living room.

The girls climb inside. I look down at their four frightened faces. "We will be back for you."

"Etta, why don't you get inside with them?" Konrad asks me. I know that he is barely hanging on with all of the stuff happening around me, but I can't leave the girls to defend themselves. It's my job to protect them.

I shake my head no, lifting my arm and wiping the sweat off of my forehead. "I have to protect everyone. I will not hide." I walk to the wall and push the button, closing the hole, locking them inside.

It can only be opened from inside or someone who has the code, and only a few people have that.

I let out a deep breath, knowing that they are safe inside. "Now let's have some fun." I grin at the guys; they give me the same crazy look.

They live for this. These are the moments when they let their darkness out. I have seen it many times before and it's never good for the people their anger is directed towards.

Outside the house, I hear a car speeding and then it slides through the grass right toward us and I look at the guys, confused.

It comes to a full stop and a head peeks out of the window and I laugh. "You think you're going to have a party without me?" Butcher jumps out and I take his place in the passenger seat.

In the back are Kayla and Alisha with their own guns. "Drive," I tell Shaylin, sticking my upper body out of the sun roof, standing in the seat.

She screams at the top of her lungs. "Get them, girl!" She drives with one hand and has her pistol out in the other.

Konrad

WE STAND THERE and watch as the girls completely destroy everyone in sight. Shaylin is even trying to run them over.

"I raised a crazy fucking kid." Smiley shakes his head with that crazy-ass grin on his face.

Etta is just right, with her eating that shit up. A bullet hits the side of their vehicle and Shaylin does a sharp right, clipping the people who were shooting at us with the SUV and knocking them five feet in the air.

"I need to find Michael."

Ready or not, here I come, Michael.

16

ETTA

One by one they hit the ground. Fewer and fewer are alive. It's been an hour and now we can finally have a break without so many of them.

They are all over the property, it's fucking crazy.

I sit down into the seat to take a break from the craziness. We're parked to the side of the field at the back of the property.

I can feel all of the girls looking at me. "Are you okay, Etta?" Alisha asks from the back seat.

"I'm fine. I just hate that this happened and the girls won't think this is a safe place anymore." That is my fear—that they feel like they can be hurt anytime.

Shaylin shakes her head furiously. "They will know how hard you fought for them. We are all fighting for them to make sure they are safe. They know that."

I am touched by her words. "Thank you."

My door is wrenched open and I look at Shaylin in shock before I'm taken out of the SUV, my legs hitting the ground hard.

The girls are screaming as I'm carried off. I turn around and I almost vomit at the sight of who has me.

Michael.

Pure panic almost cripples me. I can't let him take me. I can't.

I fight with everything in me to make sure that doesn't happen. I can't let it happen. I need to protect my baby.

"Be fucking still, bitch! You are my wife!" he hisses at me, holding me even tighter, his hands digging into my arms.

I kick back, hoping to connect with his shin, my elbow digging into his stomach.

I look back at the girls, who are following at a distance. Shaylin looks terrified right now.

"KONRAD!" Kayla yells at the top of her lungs to get the guys' attention out into the field.

Michael was hiding in the fucking woods, which is why I never saw him coming. "Oh, how I am going to love getting reacquainted with you again before I kill you!" he yells into my ear.

I reach behind me and I dig my hand into his pants, grabbing his balls and squeezing with all of my might.

I grin in satisfaction at the beautiful sound of him screaming and his balls shattering in my hand.

He lifts his hand like he is going to hit me. I try to back away. I close my eyes, waiting for the punch, but it doesn't come.

Konrad

HEARING KAYLA YELLING for me had my soul leaving my fucking body. I saw right off the bat what had her screaming as Michael carried off Etta.

I reach her just as he throws a punch, I step in front of her and his fist hits me in the chest instead.

He looks at me in shock like he can't believe I'm actually standing in front of him, but oh yes.

"How I have waited to meet you, Michael." I grin at him, my hand taking the fist that dared to hit her. I lift his wrist back farther and farther toward his shoulder.

His face reddens with his pain. "Please don't break it," he begs me, but I laugh at his fucking audacity.

He looks to Etta like she's going to help him. I pull her behind me so he can't look at her. I don't want him to look at her. He is not fucking worthy of that.

I pull it back and look him dead in the fucking eyes as I do so. "You think breaking your wrist is going to be the worst thing that happens to you?"

I hear the snap and that shit runs through me, pure fucking pleasure at his scream. I grip his face. "Get used to it. I am going to break you. I am going to fucking destroy you until you wish for hell because then you may have rest, because it's not going to compare to what I do to you."

I throw him to the ground and wave for the prospects to take him from me. They drag him to one of the vans, where he will be taken to one of those fucking boxes in the basement.

I turn around and take Etta. "I am so glad you're okay, angel." I lift her face so I can kiss her. I can feel her shaking in my arms.

Her hands are on my sides. "Is it all over?" she asks me, looking into my eyes, and I smile, kissing her forehead. I look behind her to all of my brothers standing behind me, all of us battle-worn. "Yeah, baby, it's all over."

Etta

A few Weeks Later

WE ARE HAVING A FAMILY BARBECUE. Konrad's parents are here and my family is here. I am over twelve weeks pregnant and it's time to tell everyone the good news.

Konrad has tried his best to not tell everyone, but he is such a proud dad it's practically been killing him to keep all of that in.

"Can you get the food out of the oven?" I ask his mom.

She jumps out of her seat. Konrad squeezes my hand under the table. He is trying to hide his grin and pretend to be busy so no one suspects anything.

A few moments later, she comes back into the dining room holding a bun, looking confused. "Why is there a bun in the oven?" She looks at it and then at me.

She looks to me, to my stomach, then back to the bun. "Wait…" She trails off and then she screams, throwing the bun over her shoulder and running to me as fast she can, pulling me to her and hugging me.

"Oh my God! I am going to be a grandmother!" she screams, and that sets everyone in motion and running over to congratulate us.

Konrad pulls me from everyone until I am facing him. I look at him, confused as to what he's doing.

Then he gets down onto one knee in front of me.

I gasp, shocked that this is happening now. He takes my left hand. "My sweet Etta, I love you with every part of my being and I will forever until the day I am taken from this earth. Will you do me the honor of being my wife?"

"Yes!" I scream. "I would love to marry you!" He slips the beautiful ring on my finger and stands up, lifting me off of the ground.

He presses his forehead against mine. "Forever and always, baby," he whispers for only me.

"I am yours always."

EPILOGUE

KONRAD

Months Later

The second our baby was born, the life I knew was changed. The second I stared into Loretta's eyes, I fell in love for the second time in my life.

The love I feel for her is something I can't even describe. Life ends and begins with that sweet angel and her momma.

I loved seeing every single change in Etta's body over the last year. I didn't like seeing her so sick from the morning sickness though.

I kiss her forehead, rubbing her slightly rounded belly that's still swollen from pregnancy as she cuddles Loretta to her chest.

She opens her eyes to look at me, full of happiness, the darkness and the shadows long gone from that night all those months ago.

It took a long time for all of the girls to recover from that. They were scared, especially the girls whose husbands were within the group, but no one who attacked the compound made it out alive that day.

"How is momma?" I ask, rubbing her stomach. Labor was hard for her. Loretta was a big baby, but she did it.

KONRAD

The door opens and Trey walks in carrying a tray. The second Trey found out Etta was having a baby, he devoted himself to taking care of her.

He was in the delivery room with me. I got to catch Loretta and it was an amazing experience, but it was one of the worst because it absolutely killed me knowing how much pain Etta was in the whole time.

"I'm still a little sore." We just got home early this morning.

Loretta weighed ten pounds and she is the chubbiest, cutest baby I have ever seen. My mom is staying with us for the next couple of days to give Etta and me an extra break.

I help Etta sit up with Loretta when Trey puts down the tray for her and I see he made her a huge breakfast. "Eat up, you need to regain your strength and you're taking a huge-ass nap after. Give me the baby."

Etta and I laugh out loud knowing the whole reason he wants her to take a nap is because he wants to cuddle Loretta.

My mom sneaks her head in the door and she eyes Trey to see if he has the baby. "It's my turn, Trey."

I have never seen him glare at anyone the way he does my mom. He leans over and gently takes her. "She is mine right now," he tells her bluntly.

My mom looks at me and then at Trey dramatically. "How dare you!" Trey slips past her with the baby and my mom chases after him, yelling the whole time about how it's her turn to hold her.

The second they're out of earshot, Etta and I burst out laughing at them. "Oh my God, that's great." She wipes under her eyes and I kiss her cheek. I love seeing her laugh.

The last few days have been rough for her. "I love you, darlin'."

She smiles at me happily. "I love you, thank you for giving me this life and our precious baby."

My heart is so fucking soft and gone for her.

I never thought someone could come along and fucking wreck me the way she has. She has completely taken my life and it's hers, forever.

"You're the one who made this life, angel. Without you I am nothing. I went over forty years without you in my life and I will never go another second without you."

She tears up and I kiss her, her tears mingling with our kiss. Love is not easy, but it's so worth it because she is worth everything.

Konrad

Two Years Later

TODAY IS the day I'm putting an end to it all, the day I tell Etta it's over. It's not, because it isn't over for me and it isn't over for him.

I push open the door, ignoring the stench that I have gotten used to over the years.

"Hello, Michael, how are you today?" I say sadistically.

He doesn't even acknowledge me. His mind left him a long time ago. He has had every bone broken in his body and he has become Liam's test subject to test out new tortures.

What he did to Etta is unforgivable and death is not something that he should have had easily, no.

He deserved so much more and he got that.

He has been here in the dark, with enough food and water to just get by like he did her. After all of the pain he caused her, he has suffered it in his own way.

I could hear him screaming from the top of the stairs, hallucinating in the dark. He's so pale that he glows.

It's time to let the shit pass now. I walk up to him, my gun pressed against his forehead. "Say hi to the devil for me, fucker."

He doesn't even blink.

I pull the trigger and he falls back on the floor in his own shit and piss. Now it's over.

I turn around and don't look back.

Inside of the house I built for us, Etta is in the kitchen feeding Loretta her dinner and she turns around when she hears me walking in.

I smile at her little baby bump. I press my hand to it and give her a sweet kiss. "How was my girls' day?" I ask them both.

Loretta gives me a toothy grin, spaghetti sauce covering her face and all in her hair. She is the spitting image of her mother and so beautiful. "Hi Daddy." I will never grow tired of her calling me that.

"Hi Daddy," Etta repeats, and I give her a heated look that lets her know I have plans for her later.

"We have a babysitter later, Daddy." She changes her tone when she gets to *Daddy*.

"Oh really?" I reach around and squeeze her ass. I put my mouth up to her ear. "I can't wait to eat my dinner later."

I watch in satisfaction as she shivers.

Etta

THE WAIT for Trey to pick up Loretta was a killer. I handed her off and ran up the stairs, where I find Konrad sitting at the foot of the bed in a chair.

"Oh my God, this again?" I snort-laugh.

"Darlin', I am starving. Get your ass on the bed." He points and I hurry out of my clothes, lying down in front of him. "Yes, sir," I moan in anticipation.

He grips my legs, sliding me down to where he wants me. He licks his lips and gives me a wicked grin. "Now sit still and let me feast." His lips press against my inner thighs.

It's straight torture before he does exactly what I want.

Fucking bliss.

Loretta
Sixteen Years Old

"Dad! I need some money." I shush Dylan behind me, banging on their bedroom door once again for them to answer.

Dad swings open the door and gives me a stink eye. "Where do you think you're going, lady, at this hour?"

I smile, giving him my best smile that lets me get away with a lot of things. "Me and some of the kids are going to the movies. They're outside right now."

He walks to the window and looks out to see who I am talking about. I try not to roll my eyes because I only hang out with the rest of the MC kids.

He reaches into his pocket and hands me a hundred. "Don't come back until midnight." Then he walks into the bedroom once again and I hear mom squealing with laughter.

Dylan looks like he's going to throw up and I feel exactly the same way, but I do hope that one day I find love like the love my parents have.

Author note: Don't worry, she finds the love of her life and her dad definitely does not approve.

You may have guessed it but Ronny and Olivia will be the first book in the next Generation Kids books.

Ronny Grim Sinners MC Next Generation Book One Coming in 2022

Next up is Lynn and Tristan <3

New series is coming - The Grim Sinners Rebels!
Gage - River coming soon

WANT MORE TO READ?
HERE ARE MY OTHER WORKS!
<u>Forever Series</u>

Protecting His Forever

Loving His Forever

Cherishing His Forever

<u>Devil Souls MC Series</u>

Torch

Techy

Butcher

Liam

Kyle, Ryan, Jack Boxset Novella

Grim Sinners MC Series

Lane

Wilder

Travis

Aiden

Derek

Grim Sinners Originals
Smiley
Maverick

This series is under my paranormal pen name:

Teagan Wilde

Raleigh Texas Wolves

Damon
Brantley - Coming Soon

WANT TO READ A SNEAK PEEK OF THE FIRST BOOK IN THE SERIES?

SMILEY'S

ADELINE

I never expected my life to turn out this way. My daughter and I were trapped in the middle of nowhere, living with pimps and drug dealers. Her father was a piece of shit, a piece of shit I was forced into living with as a means of survival.

The moment I hit age eighteen, I'd been kicked out of the house. No money, no belongings, and stuck in the middle of nowhere, surrounded by people who wanted me to be their next whore. I couldn't do that.

This was selfish of me, but this older guy had been after me for years, and I had nowhere else to go. I knocked on his door, and that's the worst thing I've done in my entire life.

My life was never the same after that. I became the one thing I'd never wanted to be: a prostitute. My life was completely controlled by him. I lived in fear, and I wanted out so bad. I hated him so much—I hated my life. I also became pregnant. And when my daughter was older, around the time she should have started school, he began to scream at her and threaten her.

I would not let that stand; I loved my daughter more than

life itself. She deserved more than the life she'd been dealt. She was way too sweet for the world she was living in.

We were two hours outside of civilization. For years I saved up what little I could find; it would be enough to get us into town.

He caught me sneaking out of the house with my daughter. Alisha ran away and hid, and I took the brunt of it. Then he did the unthinkable. He injected me with drugs, and I became someone I never thought I would be. My life was taken away. He would pump so many drugs into me that I couldn't even tell you my name. Years of my life were gone in a split second.

I saw my daughter in glimpses of memory throughout the years. I wanted to reach out to her, but he would see the moment of clarity in my eyes and jab me with a needle—then I was gone again.

I overdosed so many times, and afterward I wished I had died. I was worthless, the worst mother in the whole world, because I had abandoned my daughter when I should have taken care of her. Eventually she grew up, but she was still trapped in this life.

Now I am staring at his body. He is dead, with a bullet right between his eyes. He has been dead a couple of days, and I am finally conscious enough to realize it. Pain is the first thing I feel, and the next thing is a fluttering in my chest. Hope. Pushing myself off the floor, I walk into the kitchen and check the place where I hid money oh so long ago.

Opening the cabinet, I see the money is still there. I press my hand to my mouth, crying. Crying for the first time in so long, because I am free. But Alisha is gone.

I am going to get help and get myself back to the person I used to be. Then I am going to find my daughter, if it's the last thing I ever do.

ADELINE

ONE AND A HALF YEARS LATER

When I walk into Alisha's house, she is sitting on the couch with her twin babies. Her husband, Techy, whose real name is Jordan, is sitting with them, doting on the twins. Alisha and Techy met online, and he took her away from a hopeless situation—and Techy and his group killed my husband.

I don't even want to say his name, the thought of him sickens me so much.

From the moment I met Techy, I've been so happy that my daughter knows what a real man is, and what real love is. I am so happy for her.

"Hey Mom, right on time." Alisha gives me her blinding smile, which reaches her eyes. For years I never saw that.

I smile back at her. I reach down and take a baby from her, smothering her in kisses. I have basically taken over the role of grandmother to every single member of the Devil Souls MC.

The MC has become a huge part of my family. In the beginning they were very wary of me. After all, the past couple of years had been hell. I was barely down from my high, and I couldn't remember much of my past. I did everything I possibly could to gain their trust and, over time, I did. I babysit their kids when they want a night out. I am the person they call if they are sick and need someone to help take care of them.

After missing so much of Alisha's life, I've done everything I can to be integrated into every part of her world. I have become exactly who I wanted to be.

Alisha, Jordan, and all the other MC members have this love that I never knew could exist. I'd never known men could be this way. For as long as I could remember, every single male in my life had been mean, abusive, and just a horrible person. My dad couldn't stand me because I was just another mouth to feed.

I want that kind of love more than anything else. I want to feel safe. I want to be so happy with someone that I can barely sit still. I want all of that, and I hope I can have it someday. But the most important thing is that I have my family.

The baby in my arms starts squealing with laughter, and I smile at my precious little Vanessa. Jordan sets the baby boy on the floor, helping Alisha off the couch. "Thank you so much, Ma, for watching the babies." Jordan smiles and gives me a side hug.

He lets me go and Alisha takes his place beside me. "I love you, Mom."

My heart is filled with happiness. "I love you, baby girl." I kiss her temple. She kisses both of the babies, and she and Jordan walk out the door.

I sit down, and little Joseph scoots over to the edge of the couch and lifts his arms for me to hold him. "Aww, Gigi's boy." I bend down, lifting him up and kissing his chubby cheek as I snuggle him.

They are both the sweetest little babies. I want more kids of my own someday. I want to do it over again. I want to do it right. I want to have a real family, with a husband who truly loves me. But I will never have that, and I will forever carry guilt over what my daughter went through. I wasn't strong enough to take her out of the situation we were in.

I wish that everything had been different. I wish my life had never gone down the path it did, but the life I have now is something I will be forever grateful for.

My demons haunt me. I am tormented by nightmares, and I've slept in the bathtub because the bed made me feel so vulnerable. I panic when strange men touch me in public. I get so paranoid; I expect the worst out of people. I put on a show for my family, but I am broken on the inside. And when I look at myself in the mirror, I am half disgusted by what I see. My body is scarred from my neck down, and I do everything in my power to keep that hidden.

This is my pain to bear; my daughter doesn't need to know any of the hell I went through throughout the years.

My story started out with making a horrible mistake, out of desperation, and being forced to have sex in exchange for food and a roof over my head. But my daughter is the best thing that ever happened to me. She was my life, and for six years I did everything I possibly could to be the best mother in the whole world. The split second he turned his anger on her, I was going to leave. But he injected me with so many drugs that I am not sure how I am alive. I was comatose. It was my worst nightmare coming true.

"Ba-ba." Joseph breaks me out of my thoughts, pulling on the ends of my hair and giving me a slobbery grin. I run my finger down his cheek, my tear landing on the back of my hand. One day I will be able to breathe freely.

I smile, my heart filled with hope. One day.

Later That Night

I PUT on a cheerful face for everyone but, on the inside, I just hurt. I am sitting on the edge of the bed, staring at the wall. I dread closing my eyes and knowing what I will see.

Something bangs the wall behind my head, my neighbor being a dick again. I close my eyes tightly, trying to be calm and focus on my breathing. *Everything is okay, what happened to you is over and you're a free woman.*

But I'm not. I'm afraid the people who still haunt me are alive out there, enjoying their fucked-up lives. One thing I do have to look forward to is babysitting Ryan and Myra's little girl. This is what I live for—I love kids so much. I run my hands over the blankets covering my hips, trying to soothe my nerves, something that has become a habit over the past couple of months.

When I first got clean, I never had nightmares. But as my mind cleared, horrible memories started to surface.

Stop these thoughts, Adeline! You're not usually this bad, get over it, I scold myself. I turn over onto my side, my back to the wall, and relax.

I WAKE up the next morning, my neck hurting from sleeping in a cramped bathtub with only a blanket under me. I sit up, rubbing my face, staring at the faucet. What would it be like to have one full night of sleep? If I see a doctor they will prescribe sleeping pills and, since rehab, I don't take any drugs stronger than Tylenol.

Gripping the sides of the bathtub, I push my sore and tired body off the bottom of the tub just as there is a knock on my door. My body freezes with absolute terror. My first thought is, *He has found me.*

But that's not true; he is dead. I close my eyes, shaking my head, trying to calm myself and my racing heart.

I go to the door after the second knock and peer through the peephole. I let out a huge breath when I see that it's Techy.

I unlock my many locks and pull the door open. When I see his grim expression, I know that we are going on lockdown. "A down-low lockdown?" I ask. This means there is danger and the club wants to keep everyone close.

He nods, stepping into my apartment and shutting the door behind him. I walk into my bedroom to get some clothes. "Techy, how many days do I need to pack for?" I grab my bag from under my bed.

He doesn't answer me. I peer out my bedroom door, and I don't see him. Weird.

I walk out of my room, and he is looking into the bathroom. *Please tell me that I remembered to close the shower curtain.* I twist my hands behind my back, a nervous habit. He finally looks away from the bathroom. I see sadness in his eyes.

"Adeline, why didn't you tell me you were struggling?" he says softly.

I sit on the edge of my couch. My stomach is in knots. I never wanted anyone to know that I was anything but okay.

Techy sits down beside me. "Adeline, are you okay?" He stops for a minute, touching my back. "You always seem so happy, like it radiates off of you."

I look at him. "I am happy around you guys, you make me happy. I don't want Alisha to think, for one second, that I live with these demons. And I don't want her to know about the guilt I feel over what she suffered. She doesn't need that burden."

Techy shakes his head. "You can't have this guilt inside of you, Adeline, you were a victim. I know horrible things have happened to you, but don't for one second have guilt about Alisha, it was out of your control."

I lower my head, crying, the pain in my heart easing just a

little. I never knew how much I needed to hear those words. It's like a balm over my heart.

"Thank you, Techy," I whisper. His arms are tight around me. "You're so good to my daughter."

"I love her, she is my world."

That brings a smile to my face. My life before all of this was a blur. It didn't even feel like my life; I was just going through the motions.

"Come, let's get out of here and to the club house." Techy helps me off the couch, and I walk into my bedroom. I shut the door behind me, giving me a few seconds to myself.

I look into my vanity mirror and smile at myself. I opened myself up just a little bit. I feel like this is a huge step in the right direction for me.

I feel much lighter after letting him know the guilt I struggle with. Who wouldn't feel guilty? But I am starting to realize I was a victim too. My life was stolen from me.

Not anymore.

Printed in Great Britain
by Amazon